Quaint Courtships

Howells & Alden

Editors

Contents

QUAINT COURTSHIPS

BY

Howells & Alden
Editors

Introduction

To the perverse all courtships probably are quaint; but if ever human nature may be allowed the full range of originality, it may very well be in the exciting and very personal moments of making love. Our own peculiar social structure, in which the sexes have so much innocent freedom, and youth is left almost entirely to its own devices in the arrangement of double happiness, is so favorable to the expression of character at these supreme moments, that it is wonderful there is so little which is idiosyncratic in our wooings. They tend rather to a type, very simple, very normal, and most people get married for the reason that they are in love, as if it were the most matter-of-course affair of life. They find the fact of being in love so entirely satisfying to the ideal, that they seek nothing adventitious from circumstance to heighten their tremendous consciousness.

Yet, here and there people, even American people, are so placed that they take from the situation a color of eccentricity, if they impart none to it, and the old, old story, which we all wish to have end well, zigzags to a fortunate close past juts and angles of individuality which the heroes and heroines have not willingly or wittingly thrown out. They would have chosen to arrive smoothly and uneventfully at the goal, as by far the greater majority do; and probably if they are aware of looking quaint to others in their progress, they do not like it. But it is this peculiar difference which renders them interesting and charming to the spectator. If we all love a lover, as Emerson says, it is not because of his selfish happiness, but because of the odd and unexpected chances which for the time exalt him above our experience, and endear him to our eager sympathies. In life one cannot perhaps have too little romance in affairs of the heart, or in literature too much; and in either one may be as quaint as one pleases in such affairs without being ridiculous.

W.D.H.

AN ENCORE
BY MARGARET DELAND

Accoring to Old Chester, to be romantic was just one shade less reprehensible than to put on airs. Captain Alfred Price, in all his seventy years, had never been guilty of airs, but certainly he had something to answer for in the way of romance.

However, in the days when we children used to see him pounding up the street from the post-office, reading, as he walked, a newspaper held at arm's length in front of him, he was far enough from romance. He was seventy years old, he weighed over two hundred pounds, his big head was covered with a shock of grizzled red hair; his pleasures consisted in polishing his old sextant and playing on a small mouth-harmonicon. As to his vices, it was no secret that he kept a fat black bottle in the chimney-closet in his own room; added to this, he swore strange oaths about his grandmother's nightcap. "He used to blaspheme," his daughter-in-law said, "but I said, 'Not in my presence, if you please!' So now he just says this foolish thing about a nightcap." Mrs. Drayton said that this reform would be one of the jewels in Mrs. Cyrus Price's crown; and added that she prayed that some day the Captain would give up tobacco and *rum*. "I am a poor, feeble creature," said Mrs. Drayton; "I cannot do much for my fellow men in active mission-work. But I give my prayers." However, neither Mrs. Drayton's prayers nor Mrs. Cyrus's active mission-work had done more than mitigate the blasphemy; the "rum" (which was good Monongahela whiskey) was still on hand; and as for tobacco, except when sleeping, eating, playing on his harmonicon, or dozing through one of Dr. Lavendar's sermons, the Captain smoked every moment, the ashes of his pipe or cigar falling unheeded on a vast and wrinkled expanse of waistcoat.

No; he was not a romantic object. But we girls, watching him stump past the schoolroom window to the post-office, used to whisper to each other, "Just think! *he eloped*."

There was romance for you!

To be sure, the elopement had not quite come off, but, except for the very end, it was all as perfect as a story. Indeed, the failure at the end made it all the better: angry parents, broken hearts,--only, the worst of it was, the hearts did not stay broken! He went and married somebody else; and so did she. You would have supposed she would have died. I am sure, in her place, any one of us would have died. And yet, as Lydia Wright said, "How could a young lady die for a young gentleman with ashes all over his waistcoat?"

However, when Alfred Price fell in love with Miss Letty Morris, he was not indifferent to his waistcoat, nor did he weigh two hundred pounds. He was slender and ruddy-cheeked, with tossing red-brown curls. If he swore, it was not by his grandmother nor her nightcap; if he drank, it was hard cider (which can often accomplish as much as "rum"); if he smoked, it was in secret, behind the stable. He wore a stock, and (on Sunday) a ruffled shirt; a high-waisted coat with two brass buttons behind, and very tight pantaloons. At that time he attended the Seminary for Youths in Upper Chester. Upper Chester was then, as in our time, the seat of learning in the township, the Female Academy being there, too. Both were boarding-schools, but the young people came home to spend Sunday; and their weekly returns, all together in the stage, were responsible for more than one Old Chester match....

"The air," says Miss, sniffing genteelly as the coach jolts past the blossoming May orchards, "is most agreeably perfumed. And how fair is the prospect from this hilltop!"

"Fair indeed!" responded her companion, staring boldly.

Miss bridles and bites her lip.

"I was not observing the landscape," the other explains, carefully.

In those days (Miss Letty was born in 1804, and was eighteen when she and the ruddy Alfred sat on the back seat of the coach)--in those days the conversation of Old Chester youth was more elegant than in our time. We, who went to Miss Bailey's school, were sad degenerates in the way of manners and language; at least so our elders told us. When Lydia Wright said, "Oh my, what an awful snow-storm!"

dear Miss Ellen was displeased. "Lydia," said she, "is there anything 'awe'-inspiring in this display of the elements?"

"No, 'm," faltered poor Lydia.

"Then," said Miss Bailey, gravely, "your statement that the storm is 'awful' is a falsehood. I do not suppose, my dear, that you intentionally told an untruth; it was an exaggeration. But an exaggeration, though not perhaps a falsehood, is unladylike, and should be avoided by persons of refinement." Just here the question arises: what would Miss Ellen (now in heaven) say if she could hear Lydia's Lydia, just home from college, remark--But no: Miss Ellen's precepts shall protect these pages.

But in the days when Letty Morris looked out of the coach window, and young Alfred murmured that the prospect was fair indeed, conversation was perfectly correct. And it was still decorous even when it got beyond the coach period and reached a point where Old Chester began to take notice. At first it was young Old Chester which giggled. Later old Old Chester made some comments; it was then that Alfred's mother mentioned the matter to Alfred's father. "He is young, and, of course, foolish," Mrs. Price explained. And Mr. Price said that though folly was incidental to Alfred's years, it must be checked.

"Just check it," said Mr. Price.

Then Miss Letty's mother awoke to the situation, and said, "Fy, fy, Letitia."

So it was that these two young persons were plunged in grief. Oh, glorious grief of thwarted love! When they met now, they did not talk of the landscape. Their conversation, though no doubt as genteel as before, was all of broken hearts. But again Letty's mother found out, and went in wrath to call on Alfred's family. It was decided between them that the young man should be sent away from home. "To save him," says the father. "To protect my daughter," says Mrs. Morris.

But Alfred and Letty had something to say.... It was in December; there was a snow-storm--a storm which Lydia Wright would certainly have called "awful"; but it did not interfere with true love; these two children met in the graveyard to swear undying constancy. Alfred's lantern came twinkling through the flakes, as he threaded his way across the hillside among the tombstones, and found Letty just inside the entrance, standing with her black serving-woman under a tulip-tree. The negress, chattering with cold and fright, kept plucking at the girl's pelisse; but once Alfred was at her side, Letty was indifferent to storm and ghosts. As for Alfred, he was too cast down to think of them.

"Letty, they will part us."

"No, my dear Alfred, no!"

"Yes. Yes, they will. Oh, if you were only mine!"

Miss Letty sighed.

"Will you be true to me, Letty? I am to go on a sailing-vessel to China, to be gone two years. Will you wait for me?"

Letty gave a little cry; two years! Her black woman twitched her sleeve.

"Miss Let, it's gittin' cole, honey."

"(Don't, Flora.)--Alfred, *two years!* Oh, Alfred, that is an eternity. Why, I should be--I should be twenty!"

The lantern, set on a tombstone beside them, blinked in a snowy gust. Alfred covered his face with his hands, he was shaken to his soul; the little, gay creature beside him thrilled at a sound from behind those hands.

"Alfred,"--she said, faintly; then she hid her face against his arm; "my dear Alfred, I will, if you desire it--fly with you!"

Alfred, with a gasp, lifted his head and stared at her. His slower mind had seen nothing but separation and despair; but the moment the word was said he was aflame. What! Would she? Could she? Adorable creature!

"Miss Let, my feet done get cole--"

("Flora, be still!)--Yes, Alfred, yes. I am thine."

The boy caught her in his arms. "But I am to be sent away on Monday! My angel, could you--fly, *to-morrow*?"

And Letty, her face still hidden against his shoulder, nodded.

Then, while the shivering Flora stamped, and beat her arms, and the lantern flared and sizzled, Alfred made their plans, which were simple to the point of childishness. "My own!" he said, when it was all arranged; then he held the lantern up and looked into her face, blushing and determined, with snowflakes gleaming on the curls that pushed out from under her big hood. "You will meet me at the minister's?" he said, passionately. "You will not fail me?"

"I will not fail you!" she said; and laughed joyously; but the young man's face was white.

She kept her word; and with the assistance of Flora, romantic again when her feet were warm, all went as they planned. Clothes were packed, savings-banks opened, and a chaise abstracted from the Price stable.

"It is my intention," said the youth, "to return to my father the value of the vehicle and nag, as soon as I can secure a position which will enable me to support my Lefty in comfort and fashion."

On the night of the elopement the two children met at the minister's house. (Yes, the very old Rectory to which we Old Chester children went every Saturday afternoon to Dr. Lavendar's Collect class. But of course there was no Dr. Lavendar there in those days.)

Well; Alfred requested this minister to pronounce them man and wife; but he coughed and poked the fire. "I am of age," Alfred insisted; "I am twenty-two." Then Mr. Smith said he must go and put on his bands and surplice first; and Alfred said, "If you please, sir." And off went Mr. Smith--and sent a note to Alfred's father and Letty's mother!

We girls used to wonder what the lovers talked about while they waited for the traitor. Ellen Dale always said they were foolish to wait. "Why didn't they go right off?" said Ellen. "If I were going to elope, I shouldn't bother to get married. But, oh, think of how they felt when in walked those cruel parents!"

The story was that they were torn weeping from each other's arms; that Letty was sent to bed for two days on bread and water; that Alfred was packed off to Philadelphia the very next morning, and sailed in less than a week. They did not see each other again.

But the end of the story was not romantic at all. Letty, although she crept about for a while in deep disgrace, and brooded upon death--that interesting impossibility, so dear to youth,--married, if you please! when she was twenty, and went away to live. When Alfred came back, seven years later, he got married, too. He married a Miss Barkley. He used to go away on long voyages, so perhaps he wasn't really fond of her. We tried to think so, for we liked Captain Price.

In our day Captain Price was a widower. He had given up the sea, and settled down to live in Old Chester; his son, Cyrus, lived with him, and his languid daughter-in-law--a young lady of dominant feebleness, who ruled the two men with that most powerful domestic rod--foolish weakness. This combination in a woman will cause a mountain (a masculine mountain) to fly from its firm base; while kindness, justice, and good sense leave it upon unshaken foundations of selfishness. Mrs. Cyrus was a Goliath of silliness; when billowing black clouds heaped themselves in the west on a hot afternoon, she turned pale with apprehension, and the Captain and Cyrus ran for four tumblers, into which they put the legs of her bed, where, cowering among the feathers, she lay cold with fear and perspiration. Every night the Captain screwed down all the windows on the lower floor; in the morning Cyrus pulled the screws out. Cyrus had a pretty taste in horseflesh, but Gussie cried so when he once bought a trotter that he had long ago resigned himself to a friendly beast of twenty-seven years, who could not go much out of a walk because he had string-halt in both hind legs.

But one must not be too hard on Mrs. Cyrus. In the first place, she was not born in Old Chester. But, added to that, just think of her name! The effect of names upon character is not considered as it should be. If one is called Gussie for thirty years, it is almost impossible not to become gussie after a while. Mrs. Cyrus could not be Augusta; few women can; but it was easy to be gussie--irresponsible, silly, selfish. She had a vague, flat laugh, she ate a great deal of candy, and she was afraid of--But one cannot catalogue Mrs. Cyrus's fears. They were as the sands of the sea for number. And these two men were governed by them. Only when the secrets of all hearts shall be revealed will it be understood why a man loves a fool; but why he obeys her is obvious enough: Fear is the greatest power in the world; Gussie was afraid of thunder-storms, or what not; but the Captain and Cyrus were afraid of Gussie! A hint of tears in her pale eyes, and her husband would sigh with anxiety and Captain Price slip his pipe in his pocket and sneak out of the room. Doubtless Cyrus would often have been glad to follow him, but the old gentleman glared when his son showed a desire for his company.

"Want to come and smoke with me? 'Your granny was Murray!'--you're sojering. You're first mate; you belong on the bridge in storms. I'm before the mast. Tend to your business!"

It was forty-eight years before Letty and Alfred saw each other again--or at least before persons calling themselves by those old names saw each other. Were they Letty and Alfred--this tousled, tangled, good-humored old man, ruddy and cowed, and this small, bright-eyed old lady, led about by a devoted daughter? Certainly these two persons bore no resemblance to the boy and girl torn from each other's arms that cold December night. Alfred had been mild and slow; Captain Price (except when his daughter-in-law raised her finger) was a pleasant old roaring lion. Letty had been a gay, high-spirited little creature, not as retiring, perhaps, as a young female should be, and certainly self-willed; Mrs. North was completely under the thumb of her daughter Mary. Not that "under the thumb" means unhappiness; Mary North desired only her mother's welfare, and lived fiercely for that single purpose. From morning until night (and, indeed, until morning again, for she rose often from her bed to see that there was no draught from the crack of the open window), all through the twenty-four hours she was on duty.

When this excellent daughter appeared in Old Chester and said she was going to hire a house, and bring her mother back to end her days in the home of her girlhood, Old Chester displayed a friendly interest; when she decided upon a house on Main Street, directly opposite Captain Price's, it began to recall the romance of that thwarted elopement.

"Do you suppose she knows that story about old Alfred Price and her mother?" said Old Chester; and it looked sidewise at Miss North with polite curiosity. This was not altogether because of her mother's romantic past, but because of her own manners and clothes. With painful exactness, Miss North endeavored to follow the fashion; but she looked as if articles of clothing had been thrown at her and some had stuck. As to her manners, Old Chester was divided. Mrs. Barkley said she hadn't any. Dr. Lavendar said she was shy. But, as Mrs. Drayton said, that was just like Dr. Lavendar, always making excuses for wrong-doing!--"Which," said Mrs. Drayton, "is a strange thing for a minister to do. For my part, I cannot understand impoliteness in a **Christian** female. But we must not judge," Mrs. Drayton ended, with what Willy King called her "holy look." Without wishing to "judge," it may be said that, in the matter of manners, Miss Mary North, palpitatingly anxious to be polite, told the truth. She said things that other people only thought. When Mrs. Willy King remarked that, though she did not pretend to be a good housekeeper, she had the backs of her pictures dusted every other day, Miss North, her chin trembling with shyness, said, with a panting smile:

"That's not good for housekeeping; it's foolish waste of time." Which was very rude, of course--though Old Chester was not as displeased as you might have supposed.

While Miss North, timorous and truthful (and determined to be polite), was putting the house in order before sending for her mother, Old Chester invited her to tea, and asked her many questions about Letty and the late Mr. North. But nobody asked whether she knew that her opposite neighbor, Captain Price, might have been her father;--at least that was the way Miss Ellen's girls expressed it. Captain Price himself did not enlighten the daughter he did not have; but he went rolling across the street, and pulling off his big shabby felt hat, stood at the foot of the steps, and roared out: "Morning! Anything I can do for you?" Miss North, indoors, hanging window-curtains, her mouth full of tacks, shook her head. Then she removed the tacks and came to the front door.

"Do you smoke, sir?"

Captain Price removed his pipe from his mouth and looked at it. "Why! I believe I do, sometimes," he said.

"I inquired," said Miss North, smiling tremulously, her hands gripped hard together, "because, if you do, I will ask you to desist when passing our windows."

Captain Price was so dumbfounded that for a moment words failed him. Then he said, meekly, "Does your mother object to tobacco smoke, ma'am?"

"It is injurious to all ladies' throats," said Miss North, her voice quivering and determined.

"Does your mother resemble you, madam?" said Captain Price, slowly.

"Oh no! my mother is pretty. She has my eyes, but that's all."

"I didn't mean in looks," said the old man; "she did not look in the least like you; not in the least! I mean in her views?"

"Her views? I don't think my mother has any particular views," Miss North answered, hesitatingly; "I spare her all thought," she ended, and her thin face bloomed suddenly with love.

Old Chester rocked with the Captain's report of his call; and Mrs. Cyrus told her husband that she only wished this lady would stop his father's smoking.

"Just look at his ashes," said Gussie; "I put saucers round everywhere to catch 'em, but he shakes 'em off anywhere--right on the carpet! And if you say anything, he just says, 'Oh, they'll keep the moths away!' I worry so for fear he'll set the house on fire."

Mrs. Cyrus was so moved by Miss North's active mission-work that the very next day she wandered across the street to call. "I hope I'm not interrupting you," she began, "but I thought I'd just--"

"Yes; you are," said Miss North; "but never mind; stay, if you want to." She tried to smile, but she looked at the duster which she had put down upon Mrs. Cyrus's entrance.

Gussie wavered as to whether to take offence, but decided not to;--at least not until she could make the remark which was buzzing in her small mind. It seemed strange, she said, that Mrs. North should come, not only to Old Chester, but right across the street from Captain Price!

"Why?" said Mary North, briefly.

"Why?" said Mrs. Cyrus, with faint animation. "Why, don't you know about your mother and my father-in-law?"

"Your father-in-law?--my mother?"

"Why, you know," said Mrs. Cyrus, with her light cackle, "your mother was a little romantic when she was young. No doubt she has conquered it now. But she tried to elope with my father-in-law."

"What!"

"Oh, bygones should be bygones," Mrs. Cyrus said, soothingly; "forgive and forget, you know. If there's anything I can do to assist you, ma'am, I'll send my husband over;" and then she lounged away, leaving poor Mary North silent with indignation. But that night at tea Gussie said that she thought strong-minded ladies were very unladylike; "they say she's strong-minded," she added, languidly.

"Lady!" said the Captain. "She's a man-o'-war's man in petticoats."

Gussie giggled.

"She's as thin as a lath," the Captain declared; "if it hadn't been for her face, I wouldn't have known whether she was coming bow or stern on."

"I think," said Mrs. Cyrus, "that that woman has some motive in bringing her mother back here; and *right across the street*, too!"

"What motive?" said Cyrus.

But Augusta waited for conjugal privacy to explain herself: "Cyrus, I worry so, because I'm sure that woman thinks she can catch your father again.--Oh, just listen to that harmonicon downstairs! It sets my teeth on edge!"

Then Cyrus, the silent, servile first mate, broke out: "Gussie, you're a fool!"

And Augusta cried all night, and showed herself at the breakfast-table lantern-jawed and sunken-eyed; and her father-in-law judged it wise to sprinkle his cigar ashes behind the stable.

The day that Mrs. North arrived in Old Chester, Mrs. Cyrus commanded the situation; she saw the daughter get out of the stage, and hurry into the house for a chair so that the mother might descend more easily. She also saw a little, white-haired old lady take that opportunity to leap nimbly, and quite unaided, from the swinging step.

"Now, mother!" expostulated Mary North, chair in hand, and breathless, "you might have broken your limb! Here, take my arm."

Meekly, after her moment of freedom, the little lady put her hand on that gaunt arm, and tripped up the path and into the house, where, alas! Augusta Price lost sight of them. Yet even she, with all her disapproval of strong-minded ladies, must have admired the tenderness of the man-o'-war's man. Miss North put her mother into a big chair, and hurried to bring a dish of curds.

"I'm not hungry," protested Mrs. North.

"Never mind. It will do you good."

With a sigh the little old lady ate the curds, looking about her with curious eyes. "Why, we're right across the street from the old Price house!" she said.

"Did you know them, mother?" demanded Miss North.

"Dear me, yes," said Mrs. North, twinkling; "why, I'd forgotten all about it, but the eldest boy--Now, what was his name? Al--something. Alfred,--Albert; no, Alfred. He was a beau of mine."

"Mother! I don't think it's refined to use such a word."

"Well, he wanted me to elope with him," Mrs. North said, gayly; "if that isn't being a beau, I don't know what is. I haven't thought of it for years."

"If you've finished your curds you must lie down," said Miss North.

"Oh, I'll just look about--"

"No; you are tired. You must lie down."

"Who is that stout old gentleman going into the Price house?" Mrs. North said, lingering at the window.

"Oh, that's your Alfred Price," her daughter answered; and added that she hoped her mother would be pleased with the house. "We have boarded so long, I think you'll enjoy a home of your own."

"Indeed I shall!" cried Mrs. North, her eyes snapping with delight. "Mary, I'll wash the breakfast dishes, as my mother used to do!"

"Oh no," Mary North protested; "it would tire you. I mean to take every care from your mind."

"But," Mrs. North pleaded, "you have so much to do; and--"

"Never mind about me," said the daughter, earnestly; "you are my first consideration."

"I know it, my dear," said Mrs. North, meekly. And when Old Chester came to make its call, one of the first things she said was that her Mary was such a good daughter. Miss North, her anxious face red with determination, bore out the assertion by constantly interrupting the conversation to bring a footstool, or shut a window, or put a shawl over her mother's knees. "My mother's limb troubles her," she explained to visitors (in point of modesty, Mary North did not leave her mother a leg to stand on); then she added, breathlessly, with her tremulous smile, that she wished they would please not talk too much. "Conversation tires her," she explained. At which the little, pretty old lady opened and closed her hands, and protested that she was not tired at all. But the callers departed. As the door closed behind them, Mrs. North was ready to cry.

"Now, Mary, really!" she began.

"Mother, I don't care! I don't like to say things like that, though I'm sure I always try to say them politely. But to save you I would say anything!"

"But I enjoy seeing people, and--"

"It is bad for you to be tired," Mary said, her thin face quivering still with the effort she had made; "and they sha'n't tire you while I am here to protect you." And her protection never flagged. When Captain Price called, she asked him to please converse in a low tone, as noise was bad for her mother. "He had been here a good while before I came in," she defended herself to Mrs. North, afterwards; "and I'm sure I spoke politely."

The fact was, the day the Captain came, Miss North was out. Her mother had seen him pounding up the street, and hurrying to the door, called out, gayly, in her little, old, piping voice, "Alfred--Alfred Price!"

The Captain turned and looked at her. There was just one moment's pause; perhaps be tried to bridge the years, and to believe that it was Letty who spoke to him--Letty, whom he had last seen that wintry night, pale and weeping, in the slender green sheath of a fur-trimmed pelisse. If so, he gave it up; this plump, white-haired, bright-eyed old lady, in a wide-spreading, rustling black silk dress, was not Letty. It was Mrs. North.

The Captain came across the street, waving his newspaper, and saying, "So you've cast anchor in the old port, ma'am?"

"My daughter is not at home; do come in," she said, smiling and nodding. Captain Price hesitated; then he put his pipe in his pocket and followed her into the parlor. "Sit down," she cried, gayly. "Well, *Alfred!*"

"Well,--Mrs. North!" he said; and then they both laughed, and she began to ask questions: Who was dead? Who had so and so married? "There are not many of us left," she said. "The two Ferris girls and Theophilus Morrison and Johnny Gordon--he came to see me yesterday. And Matty Dilworth; she was younger than I,--oh, by ten years. She married the oldest Barkley boy, didn't she? I hear he didn't turn out well. You married his sister, didn't you? Was it the oldest girl or the second sister?"

"It was the second--Jane. Yes, poor Jane. I lost her in fifty-five."

"You have children?" she said, sympathetically.

"I've got a boy," he said; "but he's married."

"My girl has never married; she's a good daughter,"--Mrs. North broke off with a nervous laugh; "here she is, now!"

Mary North, who had suddenly appeared in the doorway, gave a questioning sniff, and the Captain's hand sought his guilty pocket; but Miss North only said: "How do you do, sir? Now, mother, don't talk too much and get tired." She stopped and tried to smile, but the painful color came into her face. "And--if you please, Captain Price, will you speak in a low tone? Large, noisy persons exhaust the oxygen in the air, and--"

"Mary!" cried poor Mrs. North; but the Captain, clutching his old felt hat, began to hoist himself up from the sofa, scattering ashes about as he did so. Mary North compressed her lips.

"I tell my daughter-in-law they'll keep the moths away," the old gentleman said, sheepishly.

"I use camphor," said Miss North. "Flora must bring a dust-pan."

"Flora?" Alfred Price said. "Now, what's my association with that name?"

"She was our old cook," Mrs. North explained; "this Flora is her daughter. But you never saw old Flora?"

"Why, yes, I did," the old man said, slowly. "Yes. I remember Flora. Well, good-by,--Mrs. North."

"Good-by, Alfred. Come again," she said, cheerfully.

"Mother, here's your beef tea," said a brief voice.

Alfred Price fled. He met his son just as he was entering his own house, and burst into a confidence: "Cy, my boy, come aft and splice the main-brace. Cyrus, what a female! She knocked me higher than Gilroy's kite. And her mother was as sweet a girl as you ever saw!" He drew his son into a little, low-browed, dingy room at the end of the hall. Its grimy untidiness matched the old Captain's clothes, but it was his one spot of refuge in his own house; here he could scatter his tobacco ashes almost unrebuked, and play on his harmonicon without seeing Gussie wince and draw in her breath; for Mrs. Cyrus rarely entered the "cabin." "I worry so about its disorderliness that I won't go in," she used to say, in a resigned way. And the Captain accepted her decision with resignation of his own. "Crafts of your bottom can't navigate in these waters," he agreed, earnestly; and, indeed, the room was so cluttered with his belongings that voluminous hoop-skirts could not get steerage-way. "He has so much rubbish," Gussie complained; but it was precious rubbish to the old man. His chest was behind the door; a blowfish, stuffed and varnished, hung from the ceiling; two colored prints of the "Barque *Letty M.*, 800 tons," deco-rated the walls; his sextant, polished daily by his big, clumsy hands, hung over the mantelpiece, on which were many dusty treasures--the mahogany spoke of an old steering-wheel; a whale's tooth; two Chinese wrestlers, in ivory; a fan of spread-ing white coral; a conch-shell, its beautiful red lip serving to hold a loose bunch of cigars. In the chimney-breast was a little door, and the Captain, pulling his son into the room after that call on Mrs. North, fumbled in his pockets for the key. "Here," he said; ("as the Governor of North Carolina said to the Governor of South Carolina)--Cyrus, she gave her mother *beef tea!*"

But Cyrus was to receive still further enlightenment on the subject of his op-posite neighbor:

"She called him in. I heard her, with my own ears! 'Alfred,' she said, 'come in.' Cyrus, she has designs; oh, I worry so about it! He ought to be protected. He is very old, and, of course, foolish. You ought to check it at once."

"Gussie, I don't like you to talk that way about my father," Cyrus began.

"You'll like it less later on. He'll go and see her to-morrow."

"Why shouldn't he go and see her to-morrow?" Cyrus said, and added a modest bad word; which made Gussie cry. And yet, in spite of what his wife called his "blasphemy," Cyrus began to be vaguely uncomfortable whenever he saw his father put his pipe in his pocket and go across the street. And as the winter brightened into spring, the Captain went quite often. So, for that matter, did other old friends of Mrs. North's generation, who by and by began to smile at each other, and say, "Well, Alfred and Letty are great friends!" For, because Captain Price lived right across the street, he went most of all. At least, that was what Miss North said to herself with obvious common sense--until Mrs. Cyrus put her on the right track....

"What!" gasped Mary North. "But it's impossible!"

"It would be very unbecoming, considering their years," said Gussie; "but I worry so, because, you know, nothing is impossible when people are foolish; and of course, at their age, they are apt to be foolish."

So the seed was dropped. Certainly he did come very often. Certainly her mother seemed very glad to see him. Certainly they had very long talks. Mary North shivered with apprehension. But it was not until a week later that this miserable suspicion grew strong enough to find words. It was after tea, and the two ladies were sitting before a little fire. Mary North had wrapped a shawl about her mother, and given her a footstool, and pushed her chair nearer the fire, and then pulled it away, and opened and shut the parlor door three times to regulate the draught. Then she sat down in the corner of the sofa, exhausted but alert.

"If there's anything you want, mother, you'll be sure and tell me?"

"Yes, my dear."

"I think I'd better put another shawl over your limbs?"

"Oh no, indeed!"

"Are you *sure* you don't feel a draught?"

"No, Mary; and it wouldn't hurt me if I did!"

"I was only trying to make you comfortable,--"

"I know that, my dear; you are a very good daughter. Mary, I think it would be nice if I made a cake. So many people call, and--"

"I'll make it to-morrow."

"Oh, I'll make it myself," Mrs. North protested, eagerly; "I'd really enjoy--"

"Mother! Tire yourself out in the kitchen? No, indeed! Flora and I will see to it."

Mrs. North sighed.

Her daughter sighed too; then suddenly burst out: "Old Captain Price comes here pretty often."

Mrs. North nodded, pleasantly. "That daughter-in-law doesn't half take care of him. His clothes are dreadfully shabby. There was a button off his coat to-day. And she's a foolish creature."

"Foolish? she's an unladylike person!" cried Miss North, with so much feeling that her mother looked at her in mild astonishment. "And coarse, too," said Mary North; "I think married ladies are apt to be coarse. From association with men, I suppose."

"What has she done?" demanded Mrs. North, much interested.

"She hinted that he--that you--"

"Well?"

"That he came here to--to see you."

"Well, who else would he come to see? Not you!" said her mother.

"She hinted that he might want to--to marry you."

"Well,--upon my word! I knew she was a ridiculous creature, but really--!"

Mary's face softened with relief. "Of course she is foolish; but--"

"Poor Alfred! What has he ever done to have such a daughter-in-law? Mary, the Lord gives us our children; but ***Somebody Else*** gives us our in-laws!"

"Mother!" said Mary North, horrified, "you do say such things! But really he oughtn't to come so often. I'll--I'll take you away from Old Chester rather than have him bother you."

"Mary, you are just as foolish as his daughter-in-law," said Mrs. North, impatiently.

And, somehow, poor Mary North's heart sank.

Nor was she the only perturbed person in town that night. Mrs. Cyrus had a headache, so it was necessary for Cyrus to hold her hand and assure her that Willy King said a headache did not mean brain fever.

"Willy King doesn't know everything. If he had headaches like mine, he wouldn't be so sure. I am always worrying about things, and I believe my brain can't stand it. And now I've got your father to worry about!"

"Better try and sleep, Gussie. I'll put some Kaliston on your head."

"Kaliston! Kaliston won't keep me from worrying.--Oh, listen to that harmonicon!"

"Gussie, I'm sure he isn't thinking of Mrs. North."

"Mrs. North is thinking of him, which is a great deal more dangerous. Cyrus, you **must** ask Dr. Lavendar to interfere."

As this was at least the twentieth assault upon poor Cyrus's common sense, the citadel trembled.

"Do you wish me to go into brain fever before your eyes, just from worry?" Gussie demanded. "You **must** go!"

"Well, maybe, perhaps, to-morrow--"

"To-night--to-night," said Augusta, faintly.

And Cyrus surrendered.

"Look under the bed before you go," Gussie murmured.

Cyrus looked. "Nobody there," he said, reassuringly; and went on tiptoe out of the darkened, cologne-scented room. But as he passed along the hall, and saw his father in his little cabin of a room, smoking placidly, and polishing his sextant with loving hands, Cyrus's heart reproached him.

"How's her head, Cy?" the Captain called out.

"Oh, better, I guess," Cyrus said.--("I'll be hanged if I speak to Dr. Lavendar!")

"That's good," said the Captain, beginning to hoist himself up out of his chair. "Going out? Hold hard, and I'll go 'long. I want to call on Mrs. North."

Cyrus stiffened. "Cold night, sir," he remonstrated.

"'Your granny was Murray, and wore a black nightcap!'" said the Captain; "you are getting delicate in your old age, Cy." He got up, and plunged into his coat, and tramped out, slamming the door heartily behind him; for which, later, poor Cyrus got the credit. "Where you bound?"

"Oh--down-street," said Cyrus, vaguely.

"Sealed orders?" said the Captain, with never a bit of curiosity in his big, kind voice; and Cyrus felt as small as he was. But when he left the old man at Mrs. North's door, he was uneasy again. Maybe Gussie was right! Women are keener about those things than men. And his uneasiness actually carried him to Dr. Lavendar's study, where he tried to appear at ease by patting Danny.

"What's the matter with you, Cyrus?" said Dr. Lavendar, looking at him over his spectacles. (Dr. Lavendar, in his wicked old heart, always wanted to call this young man Cipher; but, so far, grace had been given him to withstand temptation.) "What's wrong?" he said.

And Cyrus, somehow, told his troubles.

At first Dr. Lavendar chuckled; then he frowned. "Gussie put you up to this, Cy--rus?" he said.

"Well, my wife's a woman," Cyrus began, "and they're keener on such matters than men; and she said perhaps you would--would--"

"What?" Dr. Lavendar rapped on the table with the bowl of his pipe, so loudly that Danny opened one eye. "Would what?"

"Well," Cyrus stammered, "you know, Dr. Lavendar, as Gussie says, 'there's no fo--'"

"You needn't finish it," Dr. Lavendar interrupted, dryly; "I've heard it before. Gussie didn't say anything about a young fool, did she?" Then he eyed Cyrus. "Or a middle-aged one? I've seen middle-aged fools that could beat us old fellows hollow."

"Oh, but Mrs. North is far beyond middle age," said Cyrus, earnestly.

Dr. Lavendar shook his head. "Well, well!" he said. "To think that Alfred Price should have such a--And yet he is as sensible a man as I know!"

"Until now," Cyrus amended. "But Gussie thought you'd better caution him. We don't want him, at his time of life, to make a mistake."

"It's much more to the point that I should caution you not to make a mistake," said Dr. Lavendar; and then he rapped on the table again, sharply. "The Captain has no such idea--unless Gussie has given it to him. Cyrus, my advice to you is to go home and tell your wife not to be a goose. I'll tell her, if you want me to?"

"Oh no, no!" said Cyrus, very much frightened. "I'm afraid you'd hurt her feelings."

"I'm afraid I should," said Dr. Lavendar.

He was so plainly out of temper that Cyrus finally slunk off, uncomforted and afraid to meet Gussie's eye, even under its bandage of a cologne-scented handkerchief.

However, he had to meet it, and he tried to make the best of his own humiliation by saying that Dr. Lavendar was shocked at such an idea. "He said father had always been so sensible; he didn't believe he would think of such a dreadful thing. And neither do I, Gussie, honestly," Cyrus said.

"But Mrs. North isn't sensible," Gussie protested, "and she'll--"

"Dr. Lavendar said 'there was no fool like a middle-aged fool,'" Cyrus agreed.

"Middle-aged! She's as old as Methuselah!"

"That's what I told him," said Cyrus.

By the end of April Old Chester smiled. How could it help it? Gussie worried so that she took frequent occasion to point out possibilities; and after the first gasp of incredulity, one could hear a faint echo of the giggles of forty-eight years before. Mary North heard it, and her heart burned within her.

"It's got to stop," she said to herself, passionately; "I must speak to his son."

But her throat was dry at the thought. It seemed as if it would kill her to speak to a man on such a subject--even to such a man as Cyrus. But, poor, shy tigress! to save her mother, what would she not do? In her pain and fright she said to Mrs. North that if that old man kept on making her uncomfortable and conspicuous, they would leave Old Chester!

Mrs. North twinkled with amusement when Mary, in her strained and quivering voice, began, but her jaw dropped at those last words; Mary was capable of carrying her off at a day's notice! The little old lady trembled with distressed reassurances; but Captain Price continued to call.

And that was how it came about that this devoted daughter, after days of exasperation and nights of anxiety, reached a point of tense determination. She would go and see the man's son, and say ... that afternoon, as she stood before the swinging glass on her high bureau, tying her bonnet-strings, she tried to think what she would say. She hoped God would give her words--polite words; "for I *must* be polite," she reminded herself desperately. When she started across the street her paisley shawl had slipped from one shoulder, so that the point dragged on the flagstones; she had split her right glove up the back, and her bonnet was jolted over sidewise; but the thick Chantilly veil hid the quiver of her chin.

Gussie met her with effusion, and Mary, striving to be polite, smiled painfully, and said,

"I don't want to see you; I want to see your husband."

Gussie tossed her head; but she made haste to call Cyrus, who came shambling along the hall from the cabin. The parlor was dark; for though it was a day of sunshine and merry May wind, Gussie kept the shutters bowed, but Cyrus could see the pale intensity of his visitor's face. There was a moment's silence, broken by a distant harmonicon.

"Mr. Price," said Mary North, with pale, courageous lips, "you must stop your father."

Cyrus opened his weak mouth to ask an explanation, but Gussie rushed in.

"You are quite right, ma'am. Cyrus worries so about it (of course we know what you refer to). And Cyrus says it ought to be checked immediately, to save the old gentleman!"

"You must stop him," said Mary North, "for my mother's sake."

"Well--" Cyrus began.

"Have you cautioned your mother?" Gussie demanded.

"Yes," Miss North said, briefly. To talk to this woman of her mother made her wince, but it had to be done. "Will you speak to your father, Mr. Price?"

"Well, I--"

"Of course he will!" Gussie broke in; "Cyrus, he is in the cabin now."

"Well, to-morrow I--" Cyrus got up and sidled towards the door. "Anyhow, I don't believe he's thinking of such a thing."

"Miss North," said Gussie, rising "I will do it."

"What, *now?*" faltered Mary North.

"Now," said Mrs. Cyrus, firmly.

"Oh," said Miss North, "I--I think I will go home. Gentlemen, when they are crossed, speak so--so earnestly."

Gussie nodded. The joy of action and of combat entered suddenly into her little soul; she never looked less vulgar than at that moment. Cyrus had disappeared.

Mary North, white and trembling, hurried out. A wheezing strain from the harmonicon followed her into the May sunshine, then ended, abruptly;--Mrs. Price had begun! On her own door-step Miss North stopped and listened, holding her breath for an outburst.... It came. A roar of laughter. Then silence. Mary North stood, motionless, in her own parlor; her shawl, hanging from one elbow, trailed behind her; her other glove had split; her bonnet was blown back and over one ear; her heart was pounding in her throat. She was perfectly aware that she had done an unheard-of thing. "But," she said, aloud, "I'd do it again. I'd do anything to protect her. But I hope I was polite?" Then she thought how courageous Mrs. Cyrus was. "She's as brave as a lion!" said Mary North. Yet had Miss North been able to stand at the Captain's door, she would have witnessed cowardice.

"Gussie, I wouldn't cry. Confound that female, coming over and stirring you up! Now don't, Gussie! Why, I never thought of--Gussie, I wouldn't cry--"

"I have worried almost to death. Pro-promise!"

"Oh, your granny was Mur--Gussie, my dear, now *don't*."

"Dr. Lavendar said you'd always been so sensible; he said he didn't see how you could think of such a dreadful thing."

"What! Lavendar? I'll thank Lavendar to mind his business!" Captain Price forgot Gussie; he spoke "earnestly." "Dog-gone these people that pry into--Oh, now, Gussie, *don't!*"

"I've worried so awfully," said Mrs. Cyrus. "Everybody is talking about you. And Dr. Lavendar is so--so angry about it; and now the daughter has charged on me as though it is my fault!--Of course, she is queer, but--"

"Queer? she's queer as Dick's hatband! Why do you listen to her? Gussie, such an idea never entered my head,--or Mrs. North's either."

"Oh yes, it has! Her daughter said that she had had to speak to her--"

Captain Price, dumbfounded, forgot his fear and burst out: "You're a pack of fools, the whole caboodle! I swear I--"

"Oh, *don't* blaspheme!" said Gussie, faintly, and staggered a little, so that all the Captain's terror returned. *If she fainted!*

"Hi, there, Cyrus! Come aft, will you? Gussie's getting white around the gills--Cyrus!"

Cyrus came, running, and between them they get the swooning Gussie to her room. Afterwards, when Cyrus tiptoed down-stairs, he found the Captain at the cabin door. The old man beckoned mysteriously.

"Cy, my boy, come in here;"--he hunted about in his pocket for the key of the cupboard;--"Cyrus, I'll tell you what happened: that female across the street came in, and told poor Gussie some cock-and-bull story about her mother and me!" The Captain chuckled, and picked up his harmonicon. "It scared the life out of Gussie," he said; then, with sudden angry gravity,--"These people that poke their noses into other people's business ought to be thrashed. Well, I'm going over to see Mrs. North." And off he stumped, leaving Cyrus staring after him, open-mouthed.

If Mary North had been at home, she would have met him with all the agonized courage of shyness and a good conscience. But she had fled out of the house, and down along the River Road, to be alone and regain her self-control.

The Captain, however, was not seeking Miss North. He opened the front door, and advancing to the foot of the stairs, called up: "Ahoy, there! Mrs. North!"

Mrs. North came trotting out to answer the summons. "Why, Alfred!" she exclaimed, looking over the banisters, "when did you come in? I didn't hear the bell ring. I'll come right down."

"It didn't ring; I walked in," said the Captain. And Mrs. North came downstairs, perhaps a little stiffly, but as pretty an old lady as you ever saw. Her white curls lay against faintly pink cheeks, and her lace cap had a pink bow on it. But she looked anxious and uncomfortable.

("Oh," she was saying to herself, "I do hope Mary's out!)--Well, Alfred?" she said; but her voice was frightened.

The Captain stumped along in front of her into the parlor, and motioned her to a seat. "Mrs. North," he said, his face red, his eye hard, "some jack-donkeys have been poking their noses (of course they're females) into our affairs; and--"

"Oh, Alfred, isn't it horrid in them?"

"Darn 'em!" said the Captain.

"It makes me mad!" cried Mrs. North; then her spirit wavered. "Mary is so foolish; she says she'll--she'll take me away from Old Chester. I laughed at first, it was so foolish. But when she said that-oh *dear!*"

"Well, but, my dear madam, say you won't go. Ain't you skipper?"

"No, I'm not," she said, dolefully. "Mary brought me here, and she'll take me away, if she thinks it best. Best for *me*, you know. Mary is a good daughter, Alfred.

I don't want you to think she isn't. But she's foolish. Unmarried women are apt to be foolish."

The Captain thought of Gussie, and sighed. "Well," he said, with the simple candor of the sea, "I guess there ain't much difference in 'em, married or unmarried."

"It's the interference makes me mad," Mrs. North declared, hotly.

"Damn the whole crew!" said the Captain; and the old lady laughed delightedly.

"Thank you, Alfred!"

"My daughter-in-law is crying her eyes out," the Captain sighed.

"Tck!" said Mrs. North; "Alfred, you have no sense. Let her cry. It's good for her!"

"Oh no," said the Captain, shocked.

"You're a perfect slave to her," cried Mrs. North.

"No more than you are to your daughter," Captain Price defended himself; and Mrs. North sighed.

"We are just real foolish, Alfred, to listen to 'em. As if we didn't know what was good for us."

"People have interfered with us a good deal, first and last," the Captain said, grimly.

The faint color in Mrs. North's cheeks suddenly deepened. "So they have," she said.

The Captain shook his head in a discouraged way; he took his pipe out of his pocket and looked at it absent-mindedly. "I suppose I can stay at home, and let 'em get over it?"

"Stay at home? Why, you'd far better--"

"What?" said the Captain, dolefully.

"Come oftener!" cried the old lady. "Let 'em get over it by getting used to it."

Captain Price looked doubtful. "But how about your daughter?"

Mrs. North quailed. "I forgot Mary," she admitted.

"I don't bother you, coming to see you, do I?" the Captain said, anxiously.

"Why, Alfred, I love to see you. If our children would just let us alone!"

"First it was our parents," said Captain Price. He frowned heavily. "According to other people, first we were too young to have sense; and now we're too old." He took out his worn old pouch, plugged some shag into his pipe, and struck a match under the mantelpiece. He sighed, with deep discouragement.

Mrs. North sighed too. Neither of them spoke for a moment; then the little old lady drew a quick breath and flashed a look at him; opened her lips; closed them with a snap; then regarded the toe of her slipper fixedly.

The Captain, staring hopelessly, suddenly blinked; then his honest red face slowly broadened into beaming astonishment and satisfaction. *"Mrs. North--"*

"Captain Price!" she parried, breathlessly.

"So long as our affectionate children have suggested it!"

"Suggested--what?"

"Let's give 'em something to cry about!"

"Alfred!"

"Look here: we are two old fools; so they say, anyway. Let's live up to their opinion. I'll get a house for Cyrus and Gussie,--and your girl can live with 'em, if she wants to!" The Captain's bitterness showed then.

"She could live here," murmured Mrs. North.

"What do you say?"

The little old lady laughed excitedly, and shook her head; the tears stood in her eyes.

"Do you want to leave Old Chester?" the Captain demanded.

"You know I don't," she said, sighing.

"She'd take you away *to-morrow*," he threatened, "if she knew I had--I had--"

"She sha'n't know it."

"Well, then, we've got to get spliced to-morrow."

"Oh, Alfred, no! I don't believe Dr. Lavendar would--"

"I'll have no dealings with Lavendar," the Captain said, with sudden stiffness; "he's like all the rest of 'em. I'll get a license in Upper Chester, and we'll go to some parson there."

Mrs. North's eyes snapped; "Oh, no, no!" she protested; but in another minute they were shaking hands on it.

"Cyrus and Gussie can live by themselves," said the Captain, joyously, "and I'll get that hold cleaned out; she's kept the ports shut ever since she married Cyrus."

"And I'll make a cake! And I'll take care of your clothes; you really are dreadfully shabby;" she turned him round to the light, and brushed off some ashes. The Captain beamed. "Poor Alfred! and there's a button off! that daughter-in-law of yours can't sew any more than a cat (and she *is* a cat!). But I love to mend. Mary has saved me all that. She's such a good daughter--poor Mary. But she's unmarried, poor child."

However, it was not to-morrow. It was two or three days later that Dr. Lavendar and Danny, jogging along behind Goliath under the buttonwoods on the road to Upper Chester, were somewhat inconvenienced by the dust of a buggy that crawled up and down the hills just a little ahead. The hood of this buggy was up, upon which fact--it being a May morning of rollicking wind and sunshine--Dr. Lavendar speculated to his companion: "Daniel, the man in that vehicle is either blind and deaf, or else he has something on his conscience; in either case he won't mind our dust, so we'll cut in ahead at the watering-trough. G'on, Goliath!"

But Goliath had views of his own about the watering-trough, and instead of passing the hooded buggy, which had stopped there, he insisted upon drawing up beside it. "Now, look here," Dr. Lavendar remonstrated, "you know you're not thirsty." But Goliath plunged his nose down into the cool depths of the great iron caldron, into which, from a hollow log, ran a musical drip of water. Dr. Lavendar and Danny, awaiting his pleasure, could hear a murmur of voices from the depths of the eccentric vehicle which put up a hood on such a day; when suddenly Dr. Lavendar's eye fell on the hind legs of the other horse. "That's Cipher's trotter," he said to himself, and leaning out, cried: "Hi! Cy?" At which the other horse was drawn in with a jerk, and Captain Price's agitated face peered out from under the hood.

"Where! Where's Cyrus?" Then he caught sight of Dr. Lavendar. "'The devil and Tom Walker!'" said the Captain with a groan. The buggy backed erratically.

"Look out!" said Dr. Lavendar,--but the wheels locked.

Of course there was nothing for Dr. Lavendar to do but get out and take Goliath by the head, grumbling, as he did so, that Cyrus "shouldn't own such a spirited beast."

"I am somewhat hurried," said Captain Price, stiffly.

The old minister looked at him over his spectacles; then he glanced at the small, embarrassed figure shrinking into the depths of the buggy.

("Hullo, hullo, hullo!" he said, softly. "Well, Gussie's done it.) You'd better back a little, Captain," he advised.

"I can manage," said the Captain.

"I didn't say 'go back,'" Dr. Lavendar said, mildly.

"Oh!" murmured a small voice from within the buggy.

"I expect you need me, don't you, Alfred?" said Dr. Lavendar.

"What?" said the Captain, frowning.

"Captain," said Dr. Lavendar, simply, "if I can be of any service to you and Mrs. North, I shall be glad."

Captain Price looked at him. "Now, look here, Lavendar, we're going to do it this time, if all the parsons in--well, in the church, try to stop us!"

"I'm not going to try to stop you."

"But Gussie said you said--"

"Alfred, at your time of life, are you beginning to quote Gussie?"

"But she said you said it would be--"

"Captain Price, I do not express my opinion of your conduct to your daughter-in-law. You ought to have sense enough to know that."

"Well, why did you talk to her about it?"

"I didn't talk to her about it. But," said Dr. Lavendar, thrusting out his lower lip, "I should like to."

"We were going to hunt up a parson in Upper Chester," said the Captain, sheepishly.

Dr. Lavendar looked about, up and down the silent, shady road, then through the bordering elderberries into an orchard. "If you have your license," he said, "I have my prayer-book. Let's go into the orchard. There are two men working there we can get for witnesses,--Danny isn't quite enough, I suppose."

The Captain turned to Mrs. North. "What do you say, ma'am?" he said. She nodded, and gathered up her skirts to get out of the buggy. The two old men led their horses to the side of the road and hitched them to the rail fence; then the Captain helped Mrs. North through the elder-bushes, and shouted out to the men ploughing at the other side of the orchard. They came,--big, kindly young fellows, and stood gaping at the three old people standing under the apple-tree in the sunshine. Dr. Lavendar explained that they were to be witnesses, and the boys took off their hats.

There was a little silence, and then, in the white shadows and perfume of the orchard, with its sunshine, and drift of petals falling in the gay wind, Dr. Lavendar began.... When he came to "Let no man put asunder--" Captain Price growled in his grizzled red beard, "Nor woman, either!" But only Mrs. North smiled.

When it was over, Captain Price drew a deep breath of relief. "Well, this time we made a sure thing of it, Mrs. North!"

"Mrs. North?" said Dr. Lavendar; and then he did chuckle.

"Oh--" said Captain Price, and roared at the joke.

"You'll have to call me Letty," said the pretty old lady, smiling and blushing.

"Oh," said the Captain; then he hesitated. "Well, now, if you don't mind, I--I guess I won't call you Lefty; I'll call you Letitia?"

"Call me anything you want to," said Mrs. Price, gayly.

Then they all shook hands with each other, and with the witnesses, who found something left in their palms that gave them great satisfaction, and went back to climb into their respective buggies.

"We have shore leave," the Captain explained; "we won't go back to Old Chester for a few days. You may tell 'em, Lavendar."

"Oh, may I?" said Dr. Lavendar, blankly. "Well, good-by, and good luck!"

He watched the other buggy tug on ahead, and then he leaned down to catch Danny by the scruff of the neck.

"Well, Daniel," he said, "'if at first you don't succeed'--"

And Danny was pulled into the buggy.

A ROMANCE OF WHOOPING HARBOR
BY NORMAN DUNCAN

The trader ***Good Samaritan***--they called her the ***Cheap and Nasty*** on the Shore; God knows why! for she was dealing fairly for the fish, if something smartly--was wind-bound at Heart's Ease Cove, riding safe in the lee of the Giant's Hand: champing her anchor chain; nodding to the swell, which swept through the tickle and spent itself in the landlocked water, collapsing to quiet. It was late of a dirty night, but the schooner lay in shelter from the roaring wind; and the forecastle lamp was alight, the bogie snoring, the crew sprawling at case, purring in the light and warmth and security of the hour.... By and by, when the skipper's allowance of tea and hard biscuit had fulfilled its destiny, Tumm, the clerk, told the tale of Whooping Harbor, wherein the maid met Fate in the person of the fool from Thunder Arm; and I came down from the deck--from the black, wet wind of the open, changed to a wrathful flutter by the eternal barrier--in time to hear. And I was glad, for we know little enough of love, being blind of soul, perverse and proud; and love is strange past all things: wayward, accounting not, of infinite aspects--radiant to our vision, colorless; sombre, black as hell; but of unfailing beauty, we may be sure, had we but the eyes to see, the heart to interpret....

"We was reachin' up t' Whoopin' Harbor," said Tumm, "t' give the ***White Lily*** a night's lodgin', it bein' a wonderful windish night; clear enough, the moon sailin' a cloudy sky, but with a bank o' fog sneakin' round Cape Muggy like a fish-thief. An' we wasn't in no haste, anyhow, t' make Sinners' Tickle, for we was the first schooner down the Labrador that season, an' 'twas pick an' choose your berth for we, with a clean bill t' every head from Starvation Cove t' the Settin' Hen, so quick as the fish struck. So the skipper he says we'll hang the ol girl up t' Whoopin' Harbor 'til dawn; an' we'll all have a watch below, says he, with a cup o' tea, says he, if the cook can bile the water 'ithout burnin' it. Which was wonderful hard for the cook t' manage, look you! as the skipper, which knowed nothin' about feelin's, would never stop tellin' un: the cook bein' from Thunder Arm, a half-witted, glossy-eyed lumpfish o' the name o' Moses Shoos, born by chance and brung up likewise, as desperate a cook as ever tartured a stummick, but meanin' so wonderful well that we loved un, though he were like t' finish us off, every man jack, by the slow p'ison o' dirt.

"'Cook, you dunderhead!' says the skipper, with a wink t' the crew. 'You been an' scarched the water agin.'

"Shoos he looked like he'd give up for good on the spot--just like he **knowed** he was a fool, an' **had** knowed it for a long, long time,--sort o' like he was sorry for we an' sick of hisself.

"'Cook,' says the skipper, 'you went an' done it agin. Yes, you did! Don't you go denyin' of it. You'll kill us, cook,' says he, 'if you goes on like this. They isn't nothin' worse for the system,' says he, 'than this here burned water. The alamnacs,' says he, shakin' his finger at the poor cook, ''ll tell you **that!**

"'I 'low I did burn that water, skipper,' says the cook, 'if you says so. But I isn't got all my wits,' says he, the cry-baby; 'an' God knows I'm doin' my best!'

"'I always did allow, cook,' says the skipper, 'that God knowed more'n I ever thunk.'

"'An' I never **did** burn no water,' blubbers the cook, 'afore I shipped along o' you in this here dam' ol' flour-sieve of a **White Lily**.'

"'This here **what**?' snaps the skipper.

"'This here dam' ol' basket.'

"'Basket!' says the skipper. Then he hummed a bit o' 'Fishin' for the Maid I Loves,' 'ithout thinkin' much about the toon. 'Cook,' says he, 'I loves you. You is on'y a half-witted chance-child,' says he, 'but I loves you like a brother.'

"'Does you, skipper?' says the cook, with a grin, like the fool he was. 'I isn't by no means hatin' you, skipper,' says he. 'But I can't **help** burnin' the water,' says he, 'an' I 'low I don't want no blame for it. I'm sorry for you an' the crew,' says he, 'an' I wisht I hadn't took the berth. But when I shipped along o' you,' says he, 'I 'lowed I **could** cook. I knows I isn't able for it now,' says he, 'for you says so, skipper; but I'm doin' my best, an' I 'low if the water gets scarched,' says he, 'the galley fire's bewitched.'

"'Basket!' says the skipper. 'Ay, ay, cook,' says he. 'I just *loves* you.'

"They wasn't a man o' the crew liked t' hear the skipper say that; for, look you! the skipper didn't know nothin' about feelin's, an' the cook had more feelin's 'n a fool can make handy use of aboard a Labrador fishin'-craft. No, zur; the skipper didn't know nothin' about feelin's. I'm not wantin' t' say it about that there man, nor about no other man; for they isn't nothin' harder t' be spoke. But he *didn't;* an' they's nothin' else *to* it. There sits the ol' man, smoothin' his big red beard, singin', 'I'm Fishin' for the Maid I Loves,' while he looks at the poor cook, which was washin' up the dishes, for we was through with the mug-up. An' the devil was in his eyes--the devil was fair grinnin' in them little blue eyes. Lord! it made me sad t' see it; for I knowed the cook was in for bad weather, an' he wasn't no sort o' craft t' be out o' harbor in a gale o' wind like that.

"'Cook,' says the skipper.

"'Ay, zur?' says the cook.

"'Cook,' says the skipper, 'you ought t' get married.'

"'I on'y wisht I could,' says the cook.

"'You ought t' try, cook,' says the skipper, 'for the sake o' the crew. We'll all die,' says he, 'afore we sights of Bully Dick agin,' says he, 'if you keeps on burnin' the water. You *got* t' get married, cook, t' the first likely maid you sees on the Labrador,' says he, 't' save the crew. She'd do the cookin' for you. It 'll be the loss o' all hands,' says he, 'an you don't, This here burned water,' says he, 'will be the end of us, cook, an you keeps it up.'

"'I'd be wonderful glad t' 'blige you, skipper,' says the cook, 'an' I'd like t' 'blige all hands. 'Twon't be by my wish,' says he, 'that anybody'll die o' the grub they gets.'

"'Cook,' says the skipper, 'shake! I knows a *man*,' says he, 'when I sees one. Any man,' says he, 'that would put on the irons o' matrimony,' says he, 't' 'blige a shipmate,' says he, 'is a better man 'n me, an' I loves un like a brother.'

"Which cheered the cook up considerable.

"'Cook,' says the skipper, 'I 'pologize. Yes, I do, cook,' says he, 'I 'pologize.'

"'I isn't got no feelin' agin' matrimony,' says the cook. 'But I isn't able t' get took. I been tryin' every maid t' Thunder Arm,' says he, 'an' they isn't one,' says he, 'will wed a fool.'

"'Not one?' says the skipper.

"'Nar a one,' says the cook.

"'I'm s'prised,' says the skipper.

"'Nar a maid t' Thunder Arm,' says the cook, 'will wed a fool, an' I 'low they isn't one,' says he, 'on the Labrador.'

"'It's been done afore, cook,' says the skipper, 'an' I 'low 'twill be done agin, if the world don't come to an end t' oncet. Cook,' says he, 'I *knows* the maid t' do it.'

"The poor cook begun t' grin. 'Does you, skipper?' says he. 'Ah, skipper, no, you doesn't!' And he sort o' chuckled, like the fool he was. 'Ah, now, skipper,' says he, 'you doesn't know no maid would marry me!'"

"'Ay, b'y,' says the skipper, 'I got the girl for *you*. An' she isn't a thousand miles,' says he, 'from where that dam' ol' basket of a *White Lily* lies at anchor,' says he, 'in Whoopin' Harbor. She isn't what you'd call handsome an' tell no lie,' says he, 'but--'

"'Never you mind about that, skipper.'

"'No,' says the skipper, 'she isn't handsome, as handsome goes, even in these parts, but--'

"'Never you mind, skipper,' says the cook. 'If 'tis anything in the shape o' woman,' says he, ''twill do.'

"'I 'low that Liz Jones would take you, cook,' says the skipper. 'You ain't much on wits, but you got a good-lookin' hull; an' I 'low she'd be more'n willin' t' skipper a craft like you. You better go ashore, cook, when you gets cleaned up, an' see what she says. Tumm,' says he, 'is sort o' shipmates with Liz,' says he, 'an' I 'low he'll see you through the worst of it.'

"'Will you, Tumm?' says the cook.

"'Well,' says I, 'I'll see.

"I knowed Liz Jones from the time I fished Whoopin' Harbor with Skipper Bill Topsail in the *Love the Wind*, bein' cotched by the measles thereabouts, which she nursed me through; an' I 'lowed she *would* wed the cook if he asked her, so, thinks I, I'll go ashore with the fool t' see that she don't. No; she wasn't handsome--not Liz. I'm wonderful fond o' yarnin' o' good-lookin' maids; but I can't say much o' Liz; for Liz was so far t' l'eward o' beauty that many a time, lyin' sick there in the fo'c's'le o' the *Love the Wind*, I wished the poor girl would turn inside out, for, thinks I, the pattern might be a sight better on the other side. I *will* say she was big and well-muscled; an' muscles, t' my mind, courts enough t' make up for black eyes, but not for cross-eyes, much less for fuzzy whiskers. It ain't in my heart t' make sport o' Liz, lads; but I *will* say she had a club foot, for she was born in a gale, I'm told, when the *Preacher* was hangin' on off a lee shore 'long about Cape Harrigan, an' the sea was raisin' the devil. An', well--I hates t' say it, but--well, they called her 'Walrus Liz.' No; she wasn't handsome, she didn't have no good looks; but once you got a look into whichever one o' them cross-eyes you was able to cotch, you seen a deal more'n your own face; an' she *was* well-muscled, an' I 'low I'm goin' t' tell you so, for I wants t' name her good p'ints so well as her bad. Whatever--

"'Cook,' says I, 'I'll go along o' you.'

"With that the cook fell to on the dishes, an' 'twasn't long afore he was ready to clean hisself; which done, he was ready for the courtin'. But first he got out his dunny-bag, an' he fished in there 'til he pulled out a blue stockin', tied in a hard knot; an' from the toe o' that there blue stockin' he took a brass ring. 'I 'low,' says he, talkin' to hisself, in the half-witted way he had, 'it won't do no hurt t' give her mother's ring.' Then he begun t' cry. "Moses," says mother, "you better take the ring off my finger. It isn't no weddin'-ring," says she, "for I never was what you might call wed," says she, "but I got it from the Jew t' make believe I was; for it didn't do nobody no hurt, an' it sort o' pleased me. You better take it, Moses, b'y," says she, "for the dirt o' the grave would only spile it," says she, "an' I'm not wantin' it no more. Don't wear it at the fishin', dear," says she, "for the fishin' is wonderful hard," says she, "an' joolery don't stand much wear an' tear." 'Oh, mother!' says the cook, 'I done what you wanted!' Then the poor fool sighed an' looked up at the skipper. 'I 'low, skipper,' says he, ''t wouldn't do no hurt t' give the ring to a man's wife, would it? For mother wouldn't mind, would she?'

"The skipper didn't answer that.

"'Come, cook,' says I, 'leave us get under way,' for I couldn't stand it no longer.

"So the cook an' me put out in the punt t' land at Whoopin' Harbor, with the crew wishin' the poor cook well with their lips, but thinkin', God knows what! in their hearts. An' he was in a wonderful state o' fright. I never *seed* a man so took by scare afore. For, look you! he thunk she wouldn't have un, an' he thunk she would, an' he wisht she would, an' he wisht she wouldn't; an' by an' by he 'lowed he'd stand by, whatever come of it, 'for,' says he, 'the crew's g-g-got t' have better c-c-cookin' if I c-c-can g-g-get it. Lord! Tumm,' says he, ''tis a c-c-cold night,' says he, 'but I'm sweatin' like a p-p-porp-us!' I cheered un up so well as I could; an' by an' by we was on the path t' Liz Jones's house, up on Gray Hill, where she lived alone, her mother bein' dead an' her father shipped on a barque from St. Johns t' the West Indies. An' we found Liz sittin' on a rock at the turn o' the road, lookin' down from the hill at the **White Lily:** all alone--sittin' there in the moonlight, all alone--thinkin' o' God knows what!

"'Hello, Liz!' says I.

"'Hello, Tumm!' says she. 'What vethel'th that?'

"'That's the **White Lily,** Liz,' says I. An' here's the cook o' that there craft,' says I, 'come up the hill t' speak t' you.'

"'That's right,' says the cook. 'Tumm, you're right.'

"'T' thpeak t' *me!*' says she.

"I wisht she hadn't spoke quite that way. Lord! it wasn't nice. It makes a man feel bad t' see a woman hit her buzzom for a little thing like that.

"'Ay, Liz,' says I, 't' speak t' you. An' I'm thinkin', Liz,' says I, 'he'll say things no man ever said afore--t' you.'

"'That's right, Tumm,' says the cook. 'I wants t' speak as man t' man,' says he, 't' stand by what I says,' says he, meanin' it afore G-g-god!'

"Liz got off the rock. Then she begun t' kick at the path; an' she was lookin' down, but I 'lowed she had an eye on the cook all the time. 'For,' thinks I, 'she's sensed the thing out, like all the women.'

"'I'm thinkin',' says I, 'I'll go up the road a bit.'

"'Oh no, you won't, Tumm,' says she. 'You thtay right here. Whath the cook wantin' o' me?'

"'Well,' says the cook, 'I 'low I wants t' get married.'

"'T' get married!' says she.

"'That's right,' says he. 'Damme! Tumm,' says he, 'she got it right. T' get married,' says he, 'an' I 'low you'll do.'

"'Me?' says she.

"'You, Liz,' says he. 'I got t' get me a wife right away,' says he, 'an' they isn't nothin' else I've heared tell of in the neighborhood.'

"She begun to blow like a whale; an' she hit her buzzom with her fists, an' shivered. I 'lowed she was goin' t' fall in a fit. But. she looked away t' the moon, an' somehow that righted her.

"'You better thee me in daylight,' says she.

"'Don't you mind about that,' says he. 'You're a woman, an' a big one,' says he, 'an' that's all I'm askin' for.'

"She put a finger under his chin an' tipped his face t' the light.

"'You ithn't got all your thentheth, ith you?' says she.

"'Well,' says he, 'bein' born on Hollow eve,' says he, 'I isn't quite all there. But,' says he, 'I wisht I was. An' I can't do no more.'

"'An' you wanth t' wed me?' says she. 'Ith you sure you doth?'

"'I got mother's ring,' says the cook, 't' prove it.'

"'Tumm,' says Liz t' me, 'you ithn't wantin' t' get married, ith you?'

"'No, Liz,' says I. 'Not,' says I, 't' you.'

"'No,' says she. 'Not--t' me' She took me round the turn in the road. 'Tumm,' says she, 'I 'low I'll wed that man. I wanth t' get away from here,' says she, lookin' over the hills. 'I wanth t' get t' the Thouthern outporth, where there'th life. They ithn't no life here. An' I'm tho wonderful tired o' all thith! Tumm,' says she, 'no man ever afore athked me t' marry un, an' I 'low I better take thith one. He'th on'y a fool,' says she, 'but not even a fool ever come courtin' me, an' I 'low nobody but a fool would. On'y a fool, Tumm!' says she. 'But *I* ithn't got nothin' t' boatht of. God made me,' says she, 'an' I ithn't mad that He done it. I 'low He meant me t' take the firth man that come, an' be content. I 'low *I* ithn't got no right t' thtick up my nothe at a fool. For, Tumm,' says she, 'God made that fool, too. An', Tumm,' says she, 'I wanth thomethin' elthe. Oh, I wanth thomethin' elthe! I hateth t' tell you, Tumm,' says she, 'what it ith. But all the other maidth hath un, Tumm, an' I wanth one, too. I 'low they ithn't no woman happy without one, Tumm. An' I ithn't never had no chanth afore. No chanth, Tumm, though God knowth they ithn't nothin' I wouldn't do,' says she, 't' get what I wanth! I'll wed the fool,' says she. 'It ithn't a man I wanth tho much; no, it ithn't a man. Ith--'

"'What you wantin', Liz?' says I.

"'It ithn't a man, Tumm,' says she.

"'No?' says I. 'What is it, Liz?'

"'Ith a baby,' says she.

"God! I felt bad when she told me that...."

Tumm stopped, sighed, picked at a knot in the table. There was silence in the forecastle. The ***Good Samaritan*** was still nodding to the swell--lying safe at anchor in Heart's Ease Cove. We heard the gusts scamper over the deck and shake the rigging; we caught, in the intervals, the deep-throated roar of breakers, far off--all the noises of the gale. And Tumm picked at the knot with his clasp-knife; and we sat watching, silent, all.... And I felt bad, too, because of the maid at Whooping Harbor--a rolling waste of rock, with the moonlight lying on it, stretching from the whispering mystery of the sea to the greater desolation beyond; and an uncomely maid, wishing, without hope, for that which the hearts of women must ever desire....

"Ay," Tumm drawled, "it made me feel bad t' think o' what she'd been wantin' all them years; an' then I wished I'd been kinder t' Liz.... An', 'Tumm,' thinks I, 'you went an' come ashore t' stop this here thing; but you better let the skipper have his little joke, for t'will on'y s'prise him, an' it won't do nobody else no hurt. Here's this fool,' thinks I, 'wantin' a wife; an' he won't never have another chance. An' here's this maid,' thinks I, 'wantin' a baby; an' ***she*** won't never have another chance. 'Tis plain t' see,' thinks I, 'that God A'mighty, who made un, crossed their courses; an' I 'low, ecod!' thinks I, 'that 'twasn't a bad idea He had. If He's got to get out of it somehow,' thinks I, 'why, *I* don't know no better way. Tumm,' thinks I, 'you sheer off. Let Nature,' thinks I, 'have doo course an' be glorified.' So I looks Liz in the eye--an' says nothin'.

"'Tumm,' says she, 'doth you think he--'

"'Don't you be scared o' nothin','' says I. 'He's a lad o' good feelin's,' says I, 'an' he'll treat you the best he knows how. Is you goin' t' take un?'

"'I wathn't thinkin' o' that,' says she. 'I wathn't thinkin' o' ***not***. I wath jutht,' says she, 'wonderin'.'

"'They isn't no sense in that, Liz,' says I. 'You just wait an' find out.'

"'What'th hith name?' says she.

"'Shoos,' says I. 'Moses Shoos.'

"With that she up with her pinny an' begun t' cry like a young swile.

"'What you cryin' for, Liz?' says I.

"I 'low I couldn't tell what 'twas all about. But she was like all the women. Lord! 'tis the little things that makes un weep when it comes t' the weddin'.

"'Come, Liz,' says I, 'what you cryin' about?'

"'I lithp,' says she.

"'I knows you does, Liz,' says I; 'but it ain't nothin' t' cry about.'

"'I can't thay Joneth,' says she.

"'No,' says I; 'but you'll be changin' your name,' says I, 'an' it won't matter no more.'

"'An' if I can't say Joneth,' says she, 'I can't thay--'

"'Can't say what?' says I.

"'Can't thay Thooth!' says she.

"Lord! No more she could. An' t' say Moses Shoos! An' t' say M'issus Moses Shoos! Lord! It give me a pain in the tongue, t' think of it.

"'Jutht my luck,' says she; 'but I'll do my betht.'

"So we went back an' told the cook that he didn't have t' worry no more about gettin' a wife; an' he said he was more glad than sorry, an', says he, she'd better get her bonnet, t' go aboard an' get married right away. An' she 'lowed she didn't want no bonnet, but *would* like to change her pinny. So we said we'd as lief wait a spell, though a clean pinny wasn't *needed*. An' when she got back, the cook said he 'lowed the skipper could marry un well enough 'til we over-hauled a real parson; an' she thought so, too, for, says she, 'twouldn't be longer than fall, an' any sort of a weddin', says she, would do 'til then. An' aboard we went, the cook an' me pullin' the punt, an' she steerin'; an' the cook he crowed an' cackled all the way, like a half-witted rooster; but the maid didn't even cluck, for she was too wonderful solemn t' do anything but look at the moon.

"'Skipper,' said the cook, when we got in the fo'c's'le, 'here she is. *I* isn't afeared,' says he, 'and *she* isn't afeared; an' now I 'low we'll have you marry us.'

"Up jumps the skipper; but he was too much s'prised t' say a word.

"'An' I'm thinkin',' says the cook, with a nasty little wink, 'that they isn't a man in this here fo'c's'le,' says he, 'will *say* I'm afeared.'

"'Cook,' says the skipper, takin' the cook's hand, 'shake! I never knowed a man like you afore,' says he. 'T' my knowledge, you're the on'y man in the Labrador fleet would do it. I'm proud,' says he, 't' take the hand o' the man with nerve enough t' marry Walrus Liz o' Whoopin' Harbor.'

"The devil got in the eyes o' the cook--a jumpin' little brimstone devil, ecod!

"'Ay, lad,' says the skipper, 'I'm proud t' know the man that isn't afeared o' Walrus--'

"'Don't you call her that!' says the cook. 'Don't you do it, skipper!'

"I was lookin' at Liz. She was grinnin' in a holy sort o' way. Never seed nothin' like that afore--no, lads, not in all my life.

"'An' why not, cook?' says the skipper.

"'It ain't her name,' says the cook.

"'It ain't?' says the skipper. 'But I been sailin' the Labrador for twenty year,' says he, 'an' I ain't never heared her called nothin' but Walrus--'

"The devil got into the cook's hands then. I seed his fingers clawin' the air in a hungry sort o' way. An' it looked t' me like squally weather for the skipper.

"'Don't you do it no more, skipper,' says the cook. 'I isn't got no wits,' says he, 'an' I'm feelin' wonderful queer!'

"The skipper took a look ahead into the cook's eyes. 'Well, cook,' says he, I 'low,' says he, 'I won't.'

"Liz laughed--an' got close t' the fool from Thunder Arm. An' I seed her touch his coat-tail, like as if she loved it, but didn't dast do no more.

"'What you two goin' t' do?' says the skipper.

"'We 'lowed you'd marry us,' says the cook, ''til we come across a parson.'

"'I will,' says the skipper. 'Stand up here,' says he. 'All hands stand up!' says he. 'Tumm,' says he, 'get me the first Book you comes across.'

"I got un a Book.

"'Now, Liz,' says he, 'can you cook?'

"'Fair t' middlin',' says she. 'I won't lie.'

"''Twill do,' says he. 'An' does you want t' get married t' this here dam' fool?'

"'An it pleathe you,' says she.

"'Shoos,' says the skipper, 'will you let this woman do the cookin'?'

"'Well, skipper,' says the cook, 'I will; for I don't want nobody t' die o' my cookin' on this here v'y'ge.'

"'An' will you keep out o' the galley?' "'I 'low I'll **have** to.'

"'An', look you! cook, is you sure--is you **sure**,' says the skipper, with a shudder, lookin' at the roof, 'that you wants t' marry this here--'

"'Don't you do it, skipper!' says the cook. 'Don't you say that no more! By God!' says he, 'I'll kill you if you does!'

"'Is you sure,' says the skipper, 'that you wants t' marry this here--woman?'

"'I will.'

"'Well,' says the skipper, kissin' the Book, 'I'low me an' the crew don't care; an' we can't help it, anyhow.'

"'What about mother's ring?' says the cook. 'She might's well have that,' says he, 'if she's careful about the wear an' tear. For joolery,' says he t' Liz, 'don't stand it.'

"'It can't do no harm,' says the skipper.

"'Ith we married, thkipper?' says Liz, when she got the ring on.

"'Well,' says the skipper, 'I 'low that knot 'll hold 'til fall. For,' says he, 'I got a rope's end an' a belayin'-pin t' make it hold,' says he, 'til we gets long-side of a parson that knows more about matrimonial knots 'n me. We'll pick up your goods. Liz,' says he, 'on the s'uthard v'y'ge. An' I hopes, ol girl,' says he, 'that you'll be able t' boil the water 'ithout burnin' it.'

"'Ay, Liz. I been makin' a awful fist o' b'ilin' the water o' late.'

"She gave him one look--an' put her clean pinny to her eyes.

"'What you cryin' about?' says the cook.

"'I don't know,' says she; 'but I 'low 'tith becauthe now I knowth you **ith** a fool!'

"'She's right, Tumm,' says the cook. 'She's got it right! Bein' born on Hollow eve,' says he, 'I couldn't be nothin' else. But, Liz,' says he, 'I'm glad I got you, fool or no fool.'

"So she wiped her eyes, an' blowed her nose, an' give a little sniff, an' looked up, an' smiled.

"'I isn't good enough for you,' says the poor cook. 'But, Liz,' says he, 'if you kissed me,' says he, 'I wouldn't mind a bit. An' they isn't a man in this here fo'c's'le,' says he, lookin' around, 'that'll **say** I'd mind. Not one,' says he, with the little devil jumpin' in his eyes.

"Then she stopped cryin' for good.

"'Go ahead, Liz!' says he. 'I ain't afeared. Come on! Give us a kiss!'

"'Motheth Thooth,' says she, 'you're the firtht man ever athked me t' give un a kith!'

"She kissed un. 'Twas like a pistol-shot. An', Lord! her poor face was shin-in'...."

In the forecastle of the **Good Samaritan** we listened to the wind as it scampered over the deck; and we watched Tumm pick at the knot in the table.

"Was she happy?" I asked, at last.

"Well," he answered, with a laugh, "she sort o' got what she was wantin'. More'n she was lookin' for, I 'low. Seven o' them. An' all straight an' hearty. Ecod! sir, you never *seed* such a likely litter o' young uns. Spick an' span, ecod! from stem t' stern. Smellin' clean an' sweet; decks as white as snow; an' every nail an' knob polished 'til it made you blink t' see it. An' when I was down Thunder Arm way, last season, they was some talk *o' one o' them bein' raised for a parson!*"

I went on deck. The night was still black; but beyond--high over the open sea, hung in the depths of the mystery of night and space--there was a star.

HYACINTHUS
BY MARY E. WILKINS FREEMAN

The group was seated on the flat door-stone and the gravel walk in front of it, which crossed the green square of the Lynn front yard. On the wide flat stone, in two chairs, sat Mrs. Rufus Lynn and her opposite neighbor, Mrs. Wilford Biggs. On a chair on the gravel walk sat Mr. John Mangam, Mrs. Biggs's brother--an elderly unmarried man who lived in the village. On the step itself sat Mrs. Samson, an old lady of eighty-five, as straight as if she were sixteen, and by her side, her long body bent gracefully, her elbows resting on her knees, her chin resting in the cup of her two hands, Sarah Lynn, her great-granddaughter. Sarah Lynn was often spoken of as "pretty if she wasn't so slouchy," in Adams, the village in which she had been born and bred. Adams people were not, generally speaking, of the kind who understand the grace which may exist in utter freedom of attitude and motion.

It was a very hot evening of one of the hottest days of July, and Mrs. Rufus Lynn wore in deference to the climate a gown of white cambric with a little black sprig thereon, but nothing could excel the smoothly boned fit of it. And she did not lean back in her chair, but was as erect as the very old lady on the door-step, who was her grandmother, and who was also stiffly gowned, in a black cashmere as straightly made as if it had been armor. The influence of heredity showed strongly in the two, but in Sarah showed the intervening generation.

Sarah was a great beauty with no honor in her own country. Her long softly curved figure was surmounted by a head wound with braids of the purest flax color, and a face like a cameo. She was very fair, with the fairness of alabaster. Her mother's face had a hard blondness, pink and white, but fixed, and her great-grandmother had the same.

Mrs. Samson often glanced disapprovingly at her great-granddaughter, seated by her side in her utterly lax attitude. "Don't set so hunched up," she whispered to her in a sharp hiss. She did not want Mr. John Mangam, whom she regarded as a suitor of Sarah's, to have his attention called to the girl's defects.

But Sarah had laughed softly, and replied, quite aloud, in a languid, sweet voice, "Oh, it is so hot, grandma!"

"What if it is hot?" said the old woman. "You ain't no hotter settin' up than you be slouchin'." She still spoke in a whisper, and Sarah had only laughed and said nothing more.

As for Mrs. Wilford Biggs and her brother, Mr. John Mangam, they maintained, as always, silence. Neither of the two ever spoke, as a rule, unless spoken to. John was called a very rich man in Adams. He had gone to the far West in his youth and made money in cattle.

"And how in creation he ever made any money in cattle, a man that don't talk no more than he does, beats me," Mrs. Samson often said to her granddaughter, Mrs. Lynn. She was quite out-spoken to her about John Mangam, although never to Sarah. "It does seem as if a man would have to say somethin', to manage critters," said the old woman.

Mr. John Mangam and Mrs. Wilford Biggs grated on her nerves. She privately considered it an outrage for Mrs. Biggs to come over nearly every evening and sit and rock and say nothing, and often fall asleep, and for Mr. Mangam to do the same. It was not so much the silence as the attitude of almost injured expectancy which irritated. Both gave the effect of waiting for other people to talk to them, to tell them interesting bits of news, to ask them questions--to set them going, as it were.

Mrs. Lynn and her grandmother tried to fulfil their duty in this direction, but Sarah did not trouble herself in the least. She continued to sit bent over like a lily limp with the heat, and she stared with her two great blue eyes in her cameo face forth at the wonders of the summer night, and she had apparently very little consciousness of the people around her. Her loose white gown fell loosely around her; her white elbows were quite visible from the position in which she held her arms. Her lovely hair hung in soft loops over her ears. She was the only one who paid the slightest attention to the beauty of the night. She was filling her whole soul with it.

It was a wonderful night, and Adams was a village in which to see a wonderful night. It was flanked by a river, upon the opposite bank of which rose a gentle mountain. Above the mountain the moon was appearing with the beauty of revelation, and the tall trees made superb shadow effects. The night also was not without its voices and its fragrances. Katydids were shrilling from every thicket, and over somewhere near the river a whippoorwill was persistently calling. As for the fragrances, they were those of the dark, damp skirts and wings of the night, the evidences as loud as voices of green shrubs and flowers blooming in low wet places; but dominant above all was the scent of the lilies. One breathed in lilies to that extent that one's thought seemed fairly scented with them. It was easy enough, by looking toward the left, to see where the fragrance came from. There was evident, on the other side of a low hedge, a pale florescence of the flowers. Beyond them rose, pale likewise, the great Ware house, the largest in the village, and the oldest. Hyacinthus Ware was the sole representative of the old family known to be living. Presently the group on the Lynn door-step began to talk about him, leading up to the subject from the fragrance of the lilies.

"Them lilies is so sweet they are sickish," said the old grandmother.

"Yes, they be dreadful sickish," said Mrs. Lynn. Mrs. Wilford Biggs and Mr. Mangam, as usual, said nothing.

"Hyacinthus is home, I see," said Mrs. Lynn.

"Yes, I see him on the street t'other day," said the old woman, in her thick dialect. She sat straighter than ever as she gazed across at the garden of lilies and the great Ware house, and the cold step-stone seemed to pierce her old spinal column like a rod of steel; but she never flinched.

Mrs. Wilford Biggs and Mr. John Mangam said nothing.

"He is the handsomest man I ever saw," said Sarah Lynn, unexpectedly, in an odd, shamed, almost awed voice, as if she were speaking of a divinity.

Then for the first time Mr. John Mangam gave evidence of life. He did not speak, but he made an inarticulate noise between a grunt and a sniff.

"Well, if you call that man good-lookin'," said Mrs. Lynn, "you don't see the way I do, that's all." She looked straight at Mr. John Mangam as she spoke.

"I don't call him good-looking at all," said the old woman; "dreadful white-livered."

Sarah said nothing at all, but the face of the man, Hyacinthus Ware, was before her eyes still, as beautiful and grand as the face of a god.

"Never heerd such a name, either," said the old woman. "His mother was dreadful flowery. She had some outlandish blood. I don't know whether she was Eyetalian or Dutch."

"Her mother was Greek, I always heard," said Mrs. Lynn. "I dun'no' as I ever heard of any other Greek round these parts. I guess they don't emigrate much."

"I guess it was Greek, now you speak of it," said the old woman. "I knew she was outlandish on one side, anyhow. An' as fur callin' him good-lookin'--" She looked aggressively at her great-granddaughter, whose beautiful face was turned toward the moonlit night.

It was a long time that they sat there. It had been a very hot day, and the cool was grateful. Hardly a remark was made, except one from Mrs. Lynn that it was a blessing there were so few mosquitoes and they could sit outdoors such a night.

"I ain't heerd but one all the time I've been settin' here," said the old woman, "and I ketched him."

Sarah, the girl, continued to drink, to eat, to imbibe, to assimilate, toward her spiritual growth, the beauty of the night, the gentle slope of the mountain, the wavering wings of the shadows, the song of the river, the calls of the whippoorwill and the katydids, the perfume of the unseen green things in the wet places, and the overmastering sweetness of the lilies.

At last Mrs. Wilford Biggs arose to go, and also John Mangam. Both said they must be goin', they guessed, and that was the first remark that had been made by either of them. Mrs. Biggs moved with loose flops down the front walk, and John Mangam walked stiffly behind her. She had merely to cross the road; he had half a mile to walk to his bachelor abode.

"I should think he must be lonesome, poor man, with only that no-account housekeeper to home," said the old woman, as she also rose, with pain, of which she resolutely gave no evidence. Her poor old joints seemed to stab her, but she fought off the pain angrily. Instead she pitied with meaning John Mangam.

"It must be pretty hard for him," assented Mrs. Lynn. She also thought it would be a very good thing for her daughter to marry John Mangam.

Sarah said nothing. The old woman, after saying, like the others, that she guessed she must be goin', crept off alone across the field to her little house. She would have resented any offer to accompany her, and Mrs. Lynn arose to enter the house.

"Well, be you goin' to set there all night?" she asked, rather sharply, of Sarah. It had seemed to her that Sarah might have made a little effort to entertain Mr. John Mangam.

"No. I am coming in, mother," Sarah said. Sarah spoke differently from the others. She had had, as they expressed it in Adams, "advantages." She had, in fact, graduated from a girls' school of considerable repute. Her father had insisted upon it. Mrs. Lynn had rather rebelled against the outlay on Sarah's education. She had John Mangam in mind, and she thought that a course at the high school in Adams would fit her admirably for her life. However, she deferred to Rufus Lynn, and Sarah had her education.

The Lynn house was a large story-and-a-half cottage, the prevalent type of house in Adams. Mrs. Lynn slept in the room she had always occupied on the second floor. In hot weather Sarah slept in the bedroom opening out of the best parlor, because the other second-floor room was hot. Mrs. Lynn went up-stairs with her lamp and left Sarah to go to bed in the bedroom out of the parlor. Sarah went in there with her own little lamp, but even that room seemed stuffy. The heat of the day seemed to have become confined in the house. Sarah stood irresolute for a moment. She looked at the high mound of feather bed, at the small window at the foot, whence came scarcely a whiff of the blessed night air. Them she went back out on the door-step and again seated herself. As she sat there the scent of the lilies came more strongly than ever, and now with a curious effect. It was to the girl as if the fragrance were twining and winding about her and impelling her like leashes. All at once an impulse of yielding which was really freedom came to her. Why in the world should she not cross the little north yard, step over the low hedge, and go into that lily-garden? She knew that it would be beautiful there. She looked forth into the crystalline light and the soft plumy shade,--she would go over into the Ware garden. With all this, there was no ulterior motive. She had seen the man who lived in the house, and she admired him as one from afar, but she was a girl innocent not only in fact, but in dreams. Of course she had thought of a possible lover and husband, and that some day he might come, and she resented the supposition that John Mangam might be he, but she held even her imagination in a curious respect. While she dreamed of love, she worshipped at the same time.

When she had stepped lightly over the hedge and was moving among the lilies in the strange garden where she had no right, she was beautiful as any nymph. Now that she was in the midst of the lilies, it was as if their fragrance were a chorus sung with a violence of sweet breath in her very face. She felt exhilarated, even intoxicated, by it. She felt as if she were drawing the lilies so into herself that her own personality waned. She seemed to realize what it would be to bloom with that pale glory and exhale such sweetness for a few days. There were other flowers than lilies in the garden, but the lilies were very plentiful. There were white day-lilies, and tiger-lilies which were not sweet at all, and marvellous pink freckled ones which glistened as with drops of silver and were very fragrant. There were also low-growing spider-lilies, but those were not evident at this time of night, and the lilies-of-the-valley, of course, were all gone. There were, however, many other flowers of the old-fashioned varieties--verbenas sweet-williams, phlox, hollyhocks, mignonette, and the like. There was also a quantity of box. The garden was divided into rooms by the box, and in each room bloomed the flowers.

Sarah moved along at her will through the garden. Moving from enclosure to enclosure of box, she came, before she knew it, to the house itself. It loomed up before her a pale massiveness, with no lights in any of the windows, but on the back porch sat the owner. He sat in a high-back chair, with his head tilted back, and his eyes were closed and he seemed to be asleep, but Sarah was not quite sure. She stopped short. She became all at once horribly ashamed and shocked at what she was doing. What would he think of a girl roaming around his garden so late at night--a girl to whom he had never spoken? She was standing against a background of blooming hollyhocks. Her slender height shrank delicately away; she was like a nymph poised for flight, but she dared not even fly lest she wake the man on the porch if he were asleep, or arouse his attention were he awake.

She dared do nothing but remain perfectly still--as still as one of the tall hollyhocks behind her which were crowded with white and yellow rosettes of bloom. She had her long dress wound around her, holding it up with one hand, and the other hand and arm hung whitely at her side in the folds. She stood perfectly still and looked at the man in the porch, on whose face the moon was shining. He looked more than ever to her like something wonderful beyond common. The man had really a wonderful beauty. He was not very young, but no years could affect the classic outlines of his face, and his colorless skin was as clear and smooth as a boys. And more than anything to be remarked was the majestic serenity of his expression. He looked like a man who all his life had dominated not only other men, but himself. And there was, besides the appearance of the man, a certain fascination of mystery attached to him. Nobody in Adams knew just how or where he had spent his life. The old Ware house had been occupied for many years only by an old caretaker, who still remained. This caretaker was a man, but with all the housekeeping ability of a woman. He was never seen by Adams people except when he made his marketing expeditions. He was said to keep the house in immaculate order, and he also took care of the garden. He had always been in the Ware household, and there was a tradition that in his youth he had been a very handsome man. "As handsome as any handsome woman you ever saw," the old inhabitants said. He had come not very long before Joseph Ware, the father of Hyacinthus, had died. Joseph's wife had survived him several years. She died quite suddenly of pneumonia when still a comparatively young woman and when Hyacinthus was a boy. Then a maternal uncle had come and taken the boy away with him, to live nobody knew where nor how, until his return a few months since.

There was, of course, much curiosity in Adams concerning him, and the curiosity was not, generally speaking, of a complimentary tendency. Some young and marriageable girls esteemed him very handsome, but the majority of the people said that he was odd and stuck up, as his mother had been before him. He led a quiet life with his books, and he had a room on the ground-floor fitted up as a studio. In there he made things of clay and plaster, as the Adams people said, and curious-looking boxes were sent away by express. It was rumored that a statue by him had been exhibited in New York.

Some faces show more plainly in the moonlight, or one imagines so. Hyacinthus Ware's showed as clearly as if carved in marble. He in reality looked so like a statue that the girl standing in the enclosure of box with the background of hollyhocks had for a moment imagined that he might be one of his own statues. The eyes, either closed in sleep or appearing to be, heightened the effect.

But the girl was not now in a position to do more than tremble at the plight into which she had gotten herself. It seemed to her that no girl, certainly no girl in Adams, had ever done such a thing. Her freedom of mind now failed her. Another heredity asserted itself. She felt very much as her mother or her great-grandmother might have felt in a similar predicament. It was as horrible as dreams she had sometimes had of walking into church in her nightgear. She was sure that she must not move, and the more so because at a very slight motion of hers there had been a motion as if in response from the man on the porch. Then there was another drawback. Some roses grew behind the hollyhocks, and her skirt was caught. She had felt a little pull at her skirt when she essayed a slight tentative motion. Therefore, in order to fly she could not merely slip away; she would have to make extra motions to disentangle her dress. She therefore remained perfectly still in the attitude of shrinking and flight. She thought that her only course until the man should wake and enter the house; then she could slip away. She had not much fear of being discovered unless by motion; she stood in shadow. Besides, the man had no reason whatever to apprehend the presence of a girl in his garden at that hour, and would not be looking for her. She had an intuitive feeling that unless she moved he would not perceive her. Cramps began to assail even her untrammelled limbs. To maintain one pose so long was almost an impossible feat. She kept hoping that he would wake, that he must wake. It did not seem possible that he could sit there much longer and not wake; and yet the night was so hot--hot, probably, even in the great square rooms of the old Ware house. It was quite natural that he should prefer sleeping there in the cool out-of-door if he could, but an unreasoning rage seized upon her that he should. She rebelled against the very freedom in another which she had always coveted for herself.

And still he sat there, as white and beautiful and motionless as a statue, and still she kept her enforced attitude. She suffered tortures, but she said to herself that she would not yield, that she would not move. Rather than have that man discover her at that hour in his garden, she would suffer everything. It did not occur to her that possibly this suffering might have consequences which she did not foresee. All that she considered was a simple question of endurance; but all at once her head swam, and she sank down at the feet of the hollyhocks like a broken flower herself. She had completely lost consciousness.

When she came to herself she was lying on the back porch of the old Ware house and a pile of pillows was under her head, and she had a confused impression of vanishing woman draperies, which later on she thought she must have been mistaken about, as she knew, of course, that there was no woman there. Hyacinthus Ware himself was bending over her and fanning her with a great fan of peacock feathers, and the old caretaker had a little glass of wine on a tray. The first thing Sarah heard was Hyacinthus's voice, evenly modulated, with a curious stillness about it.

"I think if you can drink a little of this wine," he said, "you will feel better."

Sarah looked up at the face looking down at her, and all at once a conviction seized upon her that he had not been asleep at all; that he had pretended to be so, and had been enjoying himself at her expense, simply waiting to see how long she would stand there. He probably thought that she--she, Sarah Lynn--had come into his garden at midnight to see him. A sudden fury seized upon her, but when she tried to raise herself she found that she could not. Then she reached out her hand for the wine, and drank it with a fierce gulp, spilling some of it over her dress. It affected her almost instantly. She raised herself, the wine giving her strength, and she looked with a haughty anger at the man, whose expression seemed something between compassion and mocking.

"You saw me all the time," she said. "You did, I know you did, and you let me think you were asleep to see how long I would stand still there, and you think--you think--I was sitting on my door-step--I live in the next house--and it was very warm in the house, so I came out again and I smelled the lilies over the hedge, and--and--I did not think of you at all." She was quite on her feet then, and she looked at him with her head thrown back with an air of challenge. "I thought I would like to come over here in the garden," she continued, in the same angrily excusing tone, "and I did not dream of seeing any one. It was so late, I thought the house would be closed, and when I saw you I thought you were asleep."

The man began to look genuinely compassionate; the half-smile faded from his lips. "I understand," he said.

"And I thought if I moved you would wake and see me, and you were awake all the time. You knew all the time, and you waited for me to stand there and feel as I did. I never dreamed a man could be so cruel."

"I beg your pardon with all my heart," began Hyacinthus Ware.

But the girl was gone. She staggered a little as she ran, leaping over the box borders. When she was at last in her own home, with the door softly closed and locked behind her, and she was in the parlor bedroom, she could not believe that she was herself. She began to look at things differently. The influence of the intergeneration waned. She thought how her mother would never have done such a thing when she was a girl, how shocked she would be if she knew, and she herself was as shocked as her mother would have been.

It was only a week from the night of the garden episode that Mr. Ware came to make a call, and he came with the minister, who had been an old friend of his father's.

She lay awake a long time that night, thinking with angry humiliation how her mother wanted her to marry John Mangam, and she thought of Mr. Hyacinthus Ware and his polished, gentle manner, which was yet strong. Then all at once a feeling which she had never known before came over her. She saw quite plainly before her, in the moonlit dusk of the room, Hyacinthus Ware's face, and she felt that she could go down on her knees before him and worship him.

"Never was such a man," she said to herself. "Never was a man so beautiful and so good. He is not like other men."

It was not so much love as devotion which possessed her. She looked out of her little window opposite the bed, at the moonlit night, for the storm had cleared the air. She had the window open and a cool wind was blowing through the room. She looked out at the silver-lit immensity of the sky, and a feeling of exaltation came over her. She thought of Hyacinthus as she might have thought of a divinity. Love and marriage were hardly within her imagination in connection with him. But they came later.

Ware quite often called at the Lynn house. He often joined the group on the door-step in the summer nights. He often came when John Mangam occupied his usual chair in his usual place, and his graceful urbanity on such occasions seemed to make more evident the other man's stolid or stupid silence. Hyacinthus and Sarah usually had the most of the conversation to themselves, as even Mrs. Lynn and the old woman, who were not backward in speech, were at a loss to discuss many of the topics introduced. One evening, after they had all gone home, Mrs. Lynn looked fiercely at her daughter as she turned, holding her little lamp, which cast a glorifying reflection upon her face, into the parlor whence led her little bedroom.

"You are a good-for-nothin' girl," she said. "You ought to be ashamed of your-self."

"What do you mean, mother?" asked Sarah. She stood fair and white, confronting her mother, who was burning and coarse with wrath.

"You talk about things you and him know that the rest of us can't talk about. You take advantage because your father and me sent you to school where you could learn more than we could. It wasn't my fault I didn't go to school, and 'twa'n't his fault, poor man. He had to go to work and get all that money he has." By the last masculine pronoun Mrs. Lynn meant John Mangam.

Sarah had a spirit of her own, and she turned upon her mother, and for the time the two faces looked alike, being swayed with one emotion. "If," she said, "Mr. Ware and I had to regulate our conversation in order to enable Mr. Mangam to talk with us, I am sure I don't know what we could say. Mr. Mangam never talks, anyway."

"It ain't always the folks that talks that knows the most and is the best," said Mrs. Lynn. Then her face upon her daughter's turned malevolent, triumphant, and cruel. "I wa'n't goin' to tell you what I heard when I was in Mis' Ketchum's this afternoon," she said. "I thought at first I wouldn't, but now I'm goin' to."

"What do you mean, mother?" asked Sarah, in an angry voice; but she quailed.

"I thought at first I wouldn't," her mother continued, pitilessly, "but I see to-night how things are goin'."

"What do you mean by that, mother?"

"I see that you are fool enough to get to likin' a man that has got the gift of the gab, and that you think is good-lookin', and that wears clothes made in the city, better than a good honest feller that we have all known about ever since he was born, and that ain't got no outlandish blood in him, neither."

"Mother!"

"You needn't say mother that way. I ain't a fool, if I haven't been to school like some folks, and I see the way you two looked at each other to-night right before that poor man that has been comin' here steady and means honorable."

"Nobody asked or wanted him to come," said Sarah.

"Maybe you'll change your mind when you hear what I've got to tell you. And I'm goin' to tell you. ***Hyacinthus Ware has got a woman livin' over there in that house.***" Sarah turned ghastly pale, but she spoke firmly. "You mean he is married?" she said.

"I dun'no' whether he is married or not, but there is a woman livin' there."

"I don't believe a word of it."

"It don't make no odds whether you believe it or not, she's there."

"I don't believe it."

"She's been seed."

"Who has seen her."

"Abby Jane Ketchum herself, when she went round to the back door day before yesterday afternoon to ask if Mr. Ware would buy some of her soap. You know she's sellin' soap to get a prize."

"Where was the woman?"

"She was sittin' on the back porch with Mr. Ware, and she up and run when she see Abby Jane, and Mr. Ware turned as white as a sheet, and he bought all the soap Abby Jane had left to git out of it, so she's got enough to get a sideboard for a prize. And Abby Jane she kept her eyes open and she see a blind close in the south-west chamber, and that's where the woman sleeps."

"What kind of a looking woman was she?" asked Sarah, in a strange voice.

"As handsome as a picture, Abby Jane said, and she had on an awful stylish dress. Now if you want to have men like that comin' here to see you, and want to make more of them than you do of a man that you know is all right and is good and honest, you can."

There was something about the girl's face, as she turned away without a word, that smote her mother's heart. "I felt as if I had to tell you, Sarah," she said, in a voice which was suddenly changed to pity and apology.

"You did perfectly right to tell me, mother," said Sarah. When at last she got in her little bedroom she scarcely knew her own face in the glass. Hyacinthus Ware had kissed that face the night before, and ever since the memory of it had seemed like a lamp in her heart. She had met him when she was coming home from the post-office after dark, and he had kissed her at the gate and told her he loved her, and she expected, of course, to marry him. Even now she could not bring herself to entirely doubt him. "Suppose there is a woman there," she said to herself, "what does it prove?" But she felt in her inmost heart that it did prove a good deal.

She remembered just bow Hyacinthus looked when he spoke to her; there had been something almost childlike in his face. She could not believe, and yet in the face of all this evidence! If there was a woman living in the house with him, why had he kept it secret? Suddenly it occurred to her that she could go over in the garden and see for herself. It was a bright moonlight night and not yet late. If the woman was there, if she inhabited the southwest chamber, there might be some sign of her. Sarah placed her lamp on her bureau, gathered her skirts around her, and ran swiftly out into the night. She hurried stealthily through the garden. The lilies were gone, but there was still a strong breath of sweetness, a bouquet, as it were, of mignonette and verbena and sweet thyme and other fragrant blossoms, and the hollyhocks still bloomed. She went very carefully when she reached the last enclosure of box; she peeped through the tall file of hollyhocks, and there was Hyacinthus on the porch and there was a woman beside him. In fact, the woman was sitting in the old chair and Hyacinthus was at her feet, on the step, with his head in her lap. The moon shone on them; they looked as if they were carved with marble.

Sarah never knew how she got home, but she was back there in her little room and nobody knew that she had been in the Ware garden except herself. The next morning she had a talk with her mother. "Mother," said she, "if Mr. John Mangam wants to marry me why doesn't he say so?" She was fairly brutal in her manner of putting the question. She did not change color in the least. She was very pale that morning, and she stood more like her mother and her great-grandmother than herself.

Mrs. Lynn looked at her, and she was almost shocked. "Why, Sarah Lynn!" she gasped.

"I mean just what I say," said Sarah, firmly. "I want to know. John Mangam has been coming here steadily for nearly two years, and he never even says a word, much less asks me to marry him. Does he expect me to do it?"

"I suppose he thinks you might at least meet him half-way," said her mother, confusedly.

That afternoon she went over to Mrs. Wilford Biggs's, and the next night, it being John Mangam's night to call, Mrs. Biggs waylaid him as he was just about to cross the street to the Lynn house.

After a short conversation Mrs. Biggs and her brother crossed the street together, and it was not long before Mrs. Lynn asked Mrs. Biggs and the old grandmother, who had also come over, to go in the house and see her new black silk dress. Then it was that John Mangam mumbled something inarticulate, which Sarah translated into an offer of marriage. "Very well, I will marry you if you want me to, Mr. Mangam," she said. "I don't love you at all, but if you don't mind about that--"

John Mangam said nothing at all.

"If you don't mind that, I will marry you," said Sarah, and nobody would have known her voice. It was a voice to be ashamed of, full of despair and shame and pride, so wronged and mangled that her very spirit seemed violated. John Mangam said nothing then. She and the man sat there quite still, when Hyacinthus came stepping over the hedge.

Sarah found a voice when she saw him. She turned to him. "Good evening, Mr. Ware," she said, clearly. "I would like to announce my engagement to Mr. Mangam."

Hyacinthus stood staring at her. Sarah repeated her announcement. Then Hyacinthus Ware disregarded John Mangam as much as if he had been a post of the white fence that enclosed the Lynn yard. "What does it mean?" he cried.

"You have no right to ask," said she, also disregarding John Mangam, who sat perfectly still in his chair.

"No right to ask after--Sarah, what do you mean? Why have I no right to ask, after what we told each other?--and I intended to see your mother to-night. I only waited because--"

"Because you had a guest in the house," said Sarah, in a cold, low voice. Then John Mangam looked up with some show of animation. He had heard the gossip.

Hyacinthus looked at her a moment, speechless, then he left her without another word and went home across the hedge.

It was soon told in Adams that Sarah Lynn and John Mangam were to be married. Everybody agreed that it was a good match and that Sarah was a lucky girl. She went on with her wedding preparations. John Mangam came as usual and sat silently. Sometimes when Sarah looked at him and reflected that she would have to pass her life with this automaton a sort of madness seized her.

Hyacinthus she almost never saw. Once in a great while she met him on the street, and he bowed, raising his hat silently. He never made the slightest attempt at explanation.

One night, after supper, Sarah and her mother sat on the front door-step, and by and by the old grandmother came across the fields, and Mrs. Wilford Biggs across the street, and Mr. John Mangam from his own house farther down. He looked pre-occupied and worried that night, and while he was as silent as ever, yet his silence had the effect of speech.

They sat in their customary places: Mrs. Lynn and Mrs. Biggs in the chairs on the broad step-stone, Sarah and the old woman on the step, and Mr. John Mangam in his chair on the gravel path,--when a strange lady came stepping across the hedge from the Ware garden. She was not so very young, although she was undeniably very handsome, and her clothes were of a fashion never seen in Adams. She went straight up to the group on the door-step, and although she had too much poise of manner to appear agitated, it was evident that she was very eager and very much in earnest. Mrs. Lynn half arose, with an idea of giving her a chair, but there was no time, the lady began talking so at once.

"You are Miss Sarah Lynn, are you not?" she asked of Sarah, and she did not wait for a reply, "and you are going to be married to him?" and there was an unmistakable emphasis of scorn.

"I have just returned," said the lady; "I have not been in the house half an hour, and my father told me. You do not know, but the gentleman who has lived so long in the Ware house, the caretaker, is my father, and--and my mother was Hyacinthus's mother; her second marriage was secret, and he would never tell. My father and my mother were cousins. Hyacinthus never told." She turned to Sarah. "He would not even tell you, when he knew that you must have seen or heard something that made you believe otherwise, because--because of our mother. No, he would not even tell you."

She spoke again with a great impetuosity which made her seem very young, although she was not so very young. "I have been kept away all my life," she said, "all my life from here, that the memory of our mother should not suffer, and now I come to tell, myself, and you will marry my brother, whom you must love better than that gentleman. You must. Will you not? Tell me that you will," said she, "for

Hyacinthus is breaking his heart, and he loves you."

Before anything further could be said John Mangam rose, and walked rapidly down the gravel walk out of the yard and down the street.

Sarah felt dizzy. She bent lower as she sat and held her head in her two hands, and the strange lady came on the other side of her, and she was enveloped in a fragrance of some foreign perfume.

"My brother has been almost mad," she whispered in her ear, "and I have just found out what the trouble was. He would not tell on account of our mother, but poor mother is dead and gone."

Then the old woman on the other side raised her voice unexpectedly, and she spoke to her granddaughter, Mrs. Lynn. "You are a fool," said she, "if you wouldn't rather hev Serrah merry a man like Hyacinthus Ware, with all his money and livin' in the biggest house in Adams, than a man like John Mangam, who sets an' sets an' sets the hull evenin' and never opens his mouth to say boo to a goose, and beside bein' threatened with a suit for breach."

"I don't care who she marries, as long as she is happy," said Sarah's mother.

"Well, I'm goin'," said the old woman. "I left my winders open, and I think there's a shower comin' up."

She rose, and Mrs. Wilford Biggs at the same time. Sarah's mother went into the house.

"Won't you?" whispered the strange lady, and it was as if a rose whispered in Sarah's ear.

"I didn't know that he--I thought--" stammered Sarah.

Sarah did not exactly know when the lady left and when Hyacinthus came, but after a while they were sitting side by side on the door-step, and the moon was rising over the mountain, and the wonderful shadows were gathering about them like a company of wedding-guests.

JANE'S GRAY EYES
BY SEWELL FORD

When *The Insurgent* took its place among the "best six sellers," Decatur Brown formed several good resolutions. He would not have himself photographed in a literary pose, holding a book on his knee, or propping his forehead up with one hand and gazing dreamily into space; he would not accept the praise of newspaper reviewers as laurel dropped from Olympus; and he would not tell "how he wrote it."

Firmly he held to this commendable programme, despite frequent urgings to depart from it. Yet observe what pitfalls beset the path of the popular fictionist. There came a breezy, shrewd-eyed young woman of beguiling tongue who announced herself as a "lady journalist."

"Now for goodness' sake don't shy," she pleaded. "I'm not going to ask about your literary methods, or do a kodak write-up of the way you brush your hair, or any of that rot. I merely want you to say something about Sunday Weeks. That's legitimate, isn't it? Sunday's a public character now, you know. Every one talks about her. So why shouldn't you, who know her best?"

It was the voice of the siren. Decatur Brown should have recognized it as such. But the breezy young person was so plausible, she bubbled with such enthusiasm for his heroine, that in the end he yielded. He talked of Sunday Weeks. And such talk!

Obviously the "lady journalist" had come all primed with the rather shop-worn theory that the Sunday Weeks who figured as the heroine of *The Insurgent* must be a real personage, a young woman in whom Decatur Brown took more than a literary interest. Possibly the cards were ready to be sent out.

Had she put these queries point-blank, he would have denied them definitely and emphatically, and there would have been an end. But she was far too clever for that. She plied him with sly hints and deft insinuation. Then, when he began to scent her purpose, she took another tack. "Did he really admire women of the Sunday Weeks type? Did he honestly think that the unconventional, wilful, whimsical Sunday, while perfectly charming in the unmarried state, could be tamed to matrimony? Was he willing to have his ideal of womanhood judged by this disturbingly fascinating creature of the 'sober gray eyes and piquant chin'?"

Naturally he felt called upon to endorse his heroine, to defend her. Loyalty to his art demanded that much. Then, too, there recurred to him thoughts of Jane Temple. He could truthfully say that Sunday was a wholly imaginative character, that she had no "original." And yet subconsciously he knew that all the time he was creating her there had been before him a vision of Jane. Not a very distinct vision, to be sure. It had been some years since he had seen her. But that bit about the sober gray eyes and the piquant chin Jane was responsible for. He could never forget those eyes of Jane's. He was not so certain about the chin. It might have been piquant; and then again, it might not. At any rate, it had been adorable, for it was Jane's.

So, while some of his enthusiasm in the defence of Sunday Weeks was due to artistic fervor, more of it was prompted by thoughts of Jane Temple. He did not pretend, he declared, to speak for other men; but as for himself, he liked Sunday--he liked her very much.

The shrewd eyes of the "lady journalist" glistened. She knew her cue when she heard it. Throwing her first theory to the four winds, she eagerly gripped this new and tangible fact.

"Then she really is your ideal?"

He had not thought much about it, but he presumed that in a sense she was.

"But suppose now, Mr. Brown, just suppose you should some day run across a young woman exactly like the Sunday Weeks you have described: would you marry her?"

Decatur Brown laughed--a light, irresponsible, bachelor laugh. "I should probably ask her if I might first."

"But you *would* ask her?"

"Oh, assuredly."

"And would you like to find such a girl?"

Decatur gazed sentimentally over the smart little polo-hat of the "lady journal-ist" and out of the window at a sky--a sky as gray as Jane's eyes had been that last night when they had parted, she to travel abroad with her aunt, he to become a cub reporter on a city daily.

"Yes, I would like very much to find her," he replied.

Do you think, after this, that the interviewer waited for more? Not she. Leav-ing him mixed up with his daydream, she took herself off before he could retract, or modify, or in any way spoil the story.

Still, considering what she might have printed, she was really quite decent about it. Leaving out the startling head-lines, hers was a nice, readable, chatty ar-ticle. It contained no bald announcement that the author of *The Insurgent* was hunting, with matrimonial intent, for a gray-eyed prototype of Sunday Weeks. Yet that was the impression conveyed. Where was there a girl with sober gray eyes and a piquant chin who could answer to certain other specifications, duly set forth in one of the most popular novels of the day? Whoever she might be, wherever she was, she might know what to expect should she be discovered.

Having survived the first shock to his reticence, Decatur Brown was inclined to dismiss the matter with a laugh. He had been cleverly exploited, but he could not see that any great harm had been done. He supposed that he must become used to such things. Anyway, he was altogether too busy to give much thought to the incident, for he was in the middle of another novel that must be ready for the public before *The Insurgent* was forgotten.

He was yet to learn the real meaning of publicity. First there appeared an old friend, one who should have understood him too well to put faith in such an absur-dity.

"Say, Deck, you've simply got to dine with us Thursday night. My wife insists. She wants you to meet a cousin of hers--Denver girl, mighty bright, and"--this impressively--"she has gray eyes, you know."

Decatur grinned appreciatively, but he begged off. He was really very sorry to miss a gray-eyed girl, of course, but there was his work.

One by one his other friends had their little shy at him. Mayhew sent by mes-senger a huge placard reading, "Wanted, A Wife." Trevors called him up by tele-phone to advise him to see *Jupiter Belles* at once.

"Get a seat in A," he chuckled, "and take a good look at the third from the left, first row. She has gray eyes."

By the time he received Tiddler's atrocious sketch, representing the author of *The Insurgent* as a Diogenes looking for gray-eyed girls, he had ceased to smile over the thing. The joke was becoming a trifle stale.

Then the letters began to come in, post-marked from all over the country. They were all from young persons who had read *The Insurgent*, and evidently the interview; for, no matter what else was said, each missive contained the information that the writer of it possessed gray eyes. All save one. That was accompanied by a photograph on which an arrow had been drawn pointing towards the eyes. Under the arrow was naively inscribed, "Gray."

Decatur was not flattered. His dignity suffered. He felt cheapened, humiliated. The fact that the waning boom of his novel had received new impetus did not console him. His mildly serious expression gave place to a worried, injured look.

And then Mrs. Wheeler Upton swooped down on him with a demand for his appearance at one of her Saturday nights. For Decatur there was no choice. He was her debtor for so many helpful favors in the past that he could not refuse so simple a request. Yet he groaned in spirit as he viewed the prospect. Once it would have been different. Was it not in her pleasant drawing-rooms that he had been boosted from obscurity to shine among the other literary stars? Mrs. Upton knew them all. She made it her business to do so, bless the kindly heart of her, and to see that they knew each other. No wonder her library table groaned under the weight of autographed volumes.

But to face that crowd at Mrs. Wheeler Upton's meant to run a rapid-fire gauntlet of jokes about gray-eyed girls. However, go he must, and go he did.

He was not a little relieved to find so few there, and that most of them were young women. A girl often hesitates at voicing a witticism, because she is afraid, after all, that it may not be really funny. A man never doubts the excellence of his own humor. So, when a quarter of an hour had passed without hint of that threadbare topic, he gradually threw off his restraint and began to enjoy himself. He was talking Meredith to a tall girl in soft-blue China silk, when suddenly he became aware that they had been left entirely to themselves. Every one else seemed to have drifted into an adjoining room. Through the doorway he could see them about Mrs.

Upton, who was evidently holding their attention.

"Why, what's up, I wonder? Why do they leave us out, I'd like to know?" and he glanced inquiringly at the girl in soft blue. She flushed consciously and dropped her lashes. When she looked at him again, and rather appealingly, he saw that she had gray eyes.

It was Decatur's turn to flush. Could Mrs. Upton have done this deliberately? He was loath to think so. The situation was awkward, and awkwardly he got himself out of it.

"I say, let's see what they're up to in there," he suggested, and marched her into the other room, wondering if he showed his embarrassment as much as she did. As he sidled away from her he determined to pick out a girl whose eyes were not gray, and to stick to her for the remainder of the evening. Accordingly he began his inspection. A moment later and the whole truth blazed enlighteningly upon him. They were all gray-eyed girls, every last one of them.

If he had been waiting for a climax, he was entirely satisfied. Of course it was rather silly of him to take it all so seriously, but, sitting safely in his rooms long after his panicky retreat from Mrs. Upton's collection, he could not make light of the situation. It *was* serious. He was losing sleep, appetite, and self-respect over it.

Not that he was vain enough to imagine that every gray-eyed girl in the country, or any one of them, wished to marry him. No; he was fairly modest, as men go. He suspected that the chief emotions he inspired were curiosity and mischievousness. It was the thought of what those uncounted thousands of gray-eyed girls must conceive as his attitude towards them that hurt. Why, it was almost as though he had put a matrimonial advertisement in the newspapers. When he pictured himself looked upon as assuming to be a connoisseur of a certain type of femininity he felt as keenly disgraced as if he had set himself up for an Apollo.

In next morning's mail he noted an increased number of letters from unknown gray-eyed correspondents. That settled it. Hurriedly packing a capacious kit-bag, with the uncompleted manuscript on top, he took the first train for Ocean Park. Where else could he find a more habitable solitude than Ocean Park in early June? Once previously he had gone there before the season opened, and he knew. Later on the popular big seashore resort would seethe with vacationists. They would crowd the hotels, over-flow the board walk, cover the sands, and polka-dot the ocean. But in June the sands would be deserted, the board walk untrod, the hotels empty.

And so it was. The landlord of The Empress welcomed him effusively, not as Decatur Brown, author of *The Insurgent* and seeker of an ideal girl with gray eyes, but as plain, every-day Mr. Brown, whom Providence had sent as a June guest. Decatur was thankful for it. The barren verandas were grateful in his sight. When he had been installed in a corner suite, spread out his writing things on a flat-topped table that faced the sea, filled his ink-well, and lighted his pipe, he seemed to have escaped from a threatening presence.

He could breathe freely here, thank goodness, and work. He was just settling down to it when through the open transom behind him came the sound of rustling skirts and a voice which demanded:

"But how do you suppose he found that we were here? You're certain that it was Decatur Brown, are you?"

"Oh yes, quite certain. He has changed very little. Besides, there was the name on the register."

Decatur thrilled at the music of that answering voice. There was a little quaver in it, a faint but fascinating breaking on the low notes, such as he had never heard in any voice save Jane Temple's.

"Then Mabel must not come down to dinner to-night. She must--" The rest was lost around the corner of a corridor.

What Mabel must do remained a mystery. Must she go without her dinner altogether? He hoped not, for evidently his arrival had something to do with it. Why? Decatur gave it up. Who was Mabel, anyway? The owner of the other voice he could guess at. That must be Mrs. Philo Allen, Jane's aunt Judith, the one who had carried her off to Europe and forbidden them to write to each other. But Mabel? Oh yes! He had almost forgotten that elaborately gowned miss who at sixteen had assumed such young-ladyfied airs. Mabel was Jane's young cousin, of course, the one to whom he used to take expensive bonbons, his intent being to propitiate Aunt Judith.

So they were guests at The Empress, too--Jane and her aunt and the pampered Mabel? Chiefly, however, there was Jane. The others did not matter much. Ah, here was a gray-eyed girl that he did not dread to meet. And she had not forgotten him!

An hour later he was waiting for her in the lower hallway. Luckily she came down alone, so they had the hall seat to themselves for those first few minutes. She was the same charming Jane that he had known of old. There was an added dignity in the way she carried her shapely little head, a deeper sweetness in the curve of her thin lips. Perhaps her manner was a little subdued, too; but, after all those years with Mrs. Philo Allen, why not?

"How nice of you," she was saying, "to hunt us up and surprise us in this fashion. Auntie has been expecting you at home for weeks, you know, but when Mabel's rose-cold developed she decided that we must go to the seashore, even though we did die of lonesomeness. And here we find you--or you find us. The sea air will make Mabel presentable in a day or so, we hope."

"I'm sure I hope so, too," he assented, without enthusiasm. Really, he did not see the necessity of dragging in Mabel. Nor did he understand why Mrs. Allen had expected him, or why Jane should assume that he had hunted them up. Now that she had assumed it, though, he could hardly explain that it was an accident. He asked how long they had remained abroad.

"Oh, ages! There was an age in France, while Mabel was perfecting her accent; then there was another age in Italy, where Mabel took voice-culture and the old masters; and yet another age in Germany, while Mabel struggled with the theory of music. Our year in Devon was not quite an age; we went there for the good of Mabel's complexion."

"Indeed! Has she kept those peaches-and-cream checks?"

"Ah, you must wait and see," and Jane nodded mysteriously.

"But I--" protested Decatur.

"Oh, it will be only for a day or so. Rose-colds are so hard on the eyes, you know. In the mean time perhaps you will tell us how you happened to develop into a famous author. We are immensely proud of you, of course. Aunt Judith goes hardly anywhere without a copy of *The Insurgent* in her hand. If the persons she meets have not read it, she scolds them good. And you must hear Mabel render that chapter in which Sunday runs away from the man she loves with the man she doesn't."

There they were, back to Mabel again.

"But what about yourself, Jane?" suggested Decatur.

"About me! Why, I only--Oh, here is Aunt Judith."

Yes, there was no mistaking her, nor overlooking her. She was just as colossally commanding as ever, just as imperious. At sight of her, Decatur understood Jane's position clearly. She was still the dependent niece, the obscure satellite of a star of the first magnitude. Very distinctly had Mrs. Philo Allen once explained to him this dependence of Jane's, incidentally touching on his own unlikely prospects. That had been just before she had swept Jane off to Europe with her.

All this Aunt Judith now seemed to have forgotten. In her own imperial way she greeted him graciously, inspecting him with critical but favorable eyes.

"Really, you do look quite distinguished," was her verdict, as she took his arm in her progress towards her dinner. "I am sure Mabel will say so, too."

Whereupon they reverted once more to Mabel. The maid was bathing Mabel's eyes with witch-hazel and trying to persuade her to eat a little hot soup. Such details about Mabel seemed to be regarded as of first importance. By some mysterious reasoning, too, Mrs. Allen appeared to connect them with Decatur Brown and his presence at Ocean Park.

"To-morrow night, if all goes well, you shall see her," she whispered, exultantly, in his ear, as they left the dining-hall.

Decatur was puzzled. What if he *could* see Mabel the next night? Or what if he could not? He should survive, even if the event were indefinitely postponed. What he desired just then was that Jane should accompany him on an early-evening tramp down the board walk.

"Wouldn't it be better to wait until to-morrow evening?" asked Jane. "Perhaps Mabel can go then."

"The deuce take Mabel!" He half smothered the exclamation, and Jane appeared not to hear, yielding at last to his insistence that they start at once. But it was not the kind of a talk he had hoped to have with Jane Temple. The intimate and personal ground of conversation towards which he sought to draw her she avoided as carefully as if it had been stuck with the "No Trespassing" notices. When they returned to the hotel, Decatur felt scarcely better acquainted with her than before he had found her again.

Next evening, according to schedule, Mabel appeared. She was an exquisite young woman, there was no doubt about that. She carried herself with an almost royal air which impressed even the head waiter. Her perfect figure, perfectly encased, was graceful in every long curve. Her Devon-repaired complexion was of dazzling purity, all snowy white and sea-shell pink. One could hardly imagine how even so aristocratic a malady as a rose-cold could have dared to redden slightly the tip of that classic nose.

Turning to Decatur with languid interest she murmured:

"Ah, you see I have not forgotten you, although I often do forget faces. You may sit here, if you please, and talk to me."

It was quite like being received by a sovereign, Decatur imagined. He did his best to talk, and talk entertainingly, for no other reason than that it was expected of him. At last he said something which struck the right chord. The perfect Mabel smiled approvingly at him, and he noticed for the first time that her eyes were gray. Suspiciously he glanced across the table at Jane. Was that a mocking smile on her thinly curved lips, or was it meant for kindly encouragement?

Little by little during the succeeding two days he pieced out the situation. It was not a plot exactly, unless you could dignify Mrs. Philo Allen's confident plans by such a name. But, starting with what basis Heaven only knew, she had reached the conclusion that when the author of *The Insurgent* had described Sunday Weeks he could have had in mind but one person, the one gray-eyed girl worthy of such distinction, the girl to whom he had shown such devotion but a few years before--her daughter Mabel. Then she had begun expecting him to appear. And when he had seemingly followed them to the seaside--well, what would any one naturally think? Flutteringly she had doubtless put the question to Jane, who had probably replied as she was expected to reply.

The peerless Mabel, of course, was the only one not in the secret. Anyway, she would have taken no interest in it. Her amazing egoism would have prevented that. Nothing interested Mabel acutely unless it pertained to some attribute of her own loveliness.

As for Jane Temple's view of this business, that remained an enigma. Had she grown so accustomed to her aunt Judith's estimate of Mabel that she could accept it? That was hardly possible, for Jane had a keen sense of humor. Then why should she help to throw Mabel at his head, or him at Mabel's?

Meanwhile he walked at Mabel's side, carrying her wraps, while her mother and Jane trailed judiciously in the rear. He drove out with Mabel, Mabel's mother sitting opposite and smiling at him with an air of complacent proprietorship. He stood by the piano and turned the music while Mabel executed sonatas and other things for which he had not the least appreciation. He listened to solos from *Lucia*, which Mabel sang at Jane's suggestion. Also, Jane brought forth Mabel's sketchbooks and then ostentatiously left them alone with each other.

There was much meekness in Decatur. When handled just right he was wonderfully complaisant. But after a whole week of Mabel he decided that the limit had been reached. Seizing an occasion when Mabel was in the hands of the hairdresser and manicurist, he led her mother to a secluded veranda corner and boldly plunged into an explanation.

"I have no doubt you thought it a little strange, Mrs. Allen," he began, "my appearing to follow you down here, but really--"

"There, there, Decatur, it isn't at all necessary. It was all perfectly natural and entirely proper. In fact, I quite understood."

"But I'm afraid that you--"

"Oh, but I do comprehend. We old folks are not blind. When it was a matter of those foreign gentlemen, German barons, Italian counts, Austrian princes, and so on, I was extremely particular, perhaps overparticular. Their titles are so often shoddy. But I know all about you. You come from almost as good New England stock as we do. You are talented, almost famous. Besides, your attachment is of no sudden growth. It has stood the test of years. Yes, my dear Decatur, I heartily approve of you. However"--here she rested a plump forefinger simperingly on the first of her two chins, "your fate rests with Mabel, you know."

Once or twice he had gaspingly tried to stop her, but smilingly she had waved him aside. When she ended he was speechless. Could he tell her, after all that, what a precious bore her exquisite Mabel was to him? It had been difficult enough when the situation was only a tacit one, but now that it had been definitely expressed-- well, it was proving to be a good deal like those net snares which hunters of circus animals use, the more he struggled to free himself the more he became entangled.

Abruptly, silently, he took his leave of Mrs. Allen. He feared that if he said more she might construe it as a request, that she should immediately lay his proposal before Mabel. With a despairing, haunted look he sought the board walk.

Carpenters were hammering and sawing, painters were busy in the booths, a few old ladies sat about in the sun, here and there a happy youngster dug in the sand with a tin shovel. Decatur envied them all. They were sane, rational persons, who were not likely to be interviewed and trapped into saying fool things. Their acts were not liable to be misconstrued.

Seeing a pier jutting out, he heedlessly followed it to the very end. And there, on one of the seats built for summer guests, he found Jane.

"Where is Mabel?" she asked, anxiously.

"She is having her hair done and her nails polished, I believe," said Decatur, gloomily, dropping down beside Jane. "She is being prepared, as nearly as I can gather, to receive a proposal of marriage."

"Ah! Then you--" She turned to him inquiringly.

"It appears so now," he admitted. "I have been talking to her mother."

"Oh, I see." She said it quietly, gently, in a tone of submission.

"But you don't see," he protested. "No one sees; that is, no one sees things as they really are. Do you think, Jane, that you could listen to me for a few moments without jumping at conclusions, without assuming that you know exactly what I am going to say before I have said it?"

She said that she would try.

"Then I would like to make a confession to you."

"Wouldn't it be better to--to make it first to Mabel?"

"No, it would not," he declared, doggedly. "It concerns that interview in which I was quoted as saying things about gray-eyed girls."

"Yes, I read it. We all read it."

"I guessed that much. Well, I said those things, just as I was quoted as saying them, but I did not mean all that I was credited with meaning. I want you to believe, Jane, that when I admitted my preference for gray eyes and--and all that, I was thinking of one gray-eyed girl in particular. Can you believe that?"

"Oh, I did from the very first; that is, I did as soon as Aunt Judith--"

"Never mind about Aunt Judith," interrupted Decatur, firmly. "We will get to her in time. We are talking now about that interview. You must admit, Jane, that there are many gray-eyed girls in the country; I don't know just how many, thank Heaven, but there are a lot of them. And most of them seem not only to have read that interview, but to have made a personal application of my remarks. Have you any idea what that means to me?"

"Then you think that they are all in--"

"No, no! I don't imagine there's a single one that cares a bone button for me. But each and every one of them thinks that I am in love with her, or willing to be. If she doesn't think so, her friends do. They expect me to propose on sight, simply because of what I have said about gray eyes. You doubt that? Let me tell you what occurred just before I left town: A person whom I had counted as a friend got together a whole houseful of gray-eyed girls, and then sent for me to come and make my choice. That is what drove me from the city. That is why I came to Ocean Park in June."

"But the one particular gray-eyed girl that you mentioned? How was it that you happened to--"

"It was sheer good fortune, Jane, that I found you here."

Decatur had slipped a tentative arm along the seat-back. He was leaning towards Jane, regarding her with melancholy tenderness.

"That you found me?" she said, wonderingly. "Oh, you mean that it was fortunate you found *us* here?"

"No, I don't. I mean you--y-o-u, second person singular. Haven't you guessed by this time who was the particular gray-eyed girl I had in mind?"

"Of course I have; it was Mabel, wasn't it?"

"Mabel! Oh, hang Mabel! Jane, it was you."

"Me! Why, Decatur Brown!" Either surprise or indignation rang in her tone. He concluded that it must be the latter.

"Oh, well," he said, dejectedly, "I had no right to suppose that you'd like it. It's the truth, though, and after so much misunderstanding I am glad you know it. I want you to know that it was you who inspired Sunday Weeks, if any one did. I have never mentioned this before, have not admitted it, even to myself, until now. But I realize that it is true. We have been a long time apart, but the memory of you has never faded for a day, for an hour. So, when I tried to describe the most charming girl of whom I could think, I was describing you. As I wrote, there was constantly before me the vision of your dear gray eyes, and--"

"Decatur! Look at me. Look me straight in the eyes and tell me if they are gray."

He looked. As a matter of fact, he had been looking into her eyes for several moments. Now there was something so compelling about her tone that he bent all his faculties to the task. This time he looked not with that blindness peculiar to those who love, but, for the moment, discerningly, seeingly. And they were not gray eyes at all. They were a clear, brilliant hazel.

"Why--why!" he gasped out, chokingly. "I--I have always thought of them as gray eyes."

"If that isn't just like a man!" she exclaimed, shrugging away from him. Her quarter profile revealed those thinly curved lips pursed into a most delicious pout. "You acknowledge, don't you, that they're *not* gray?" she flung at him over her shoulder--an adorable shoulder, Decatur thought.

"Oh, I admit it," he groaned.

"Then--then why don't you go away?" It was just that trembling little quaver on the low notes which spurred him on to cast the die.

"Jane," he whispered, "I don't want to go away, and I don't want you to send me. It isn't gray eyes that I care for, or ever have cared for. It's been just you, your own dear, charming self."

"No, it hasn't been. I haven't even a piquant chin."

"That doesn't matter. What is a piquant chin, anyway?"

"You ought to know; you wrote it."

"So I did, but I didn't know what it meant. I just knew that it ought to mean something charming, which you are."

"I'm not. And I am not accomplished. I don't sing, I don't play, I don't draw."

"Thanks be for that! I don't, either. But I think you are the dearest girl in the world."

At that she turned to him and smiled a little as only Jane could smile.

"You told me that once before, a long time ago, you know."

"And you have not forgotten?"

"No. I--you see--I didn't want to forget."

Had it been August, or even July, doubtless a great number of vacationists would have been somewhat shocked at what Decatur did then. But it was early June, you remember, and on the far end of the Ocean Park fishing-pier were only these two, with just the dancing blue ocean in front.

"But," she said at length, after many other and more important things had been said between them, "what will Aunt Judith say?"

"I suppose she'll think me a lucky dog--and slightly color-blind," chuckled Decatur, joyously. "But come," he went on, helping her to rise and retaining both her hands, swaying them back and forth clasped in his, as children do in the game of London Bridge,--"come," he repeated, impulsively, "while my courage is high let us go and break the news to your aunt Judith."

There was, however, no need. Looming ponderously in the middle distance of the pier's vista, a lorgnette held to her eyes, and a frozen look of horror on her ample features, was Aunt Judith herself.

A STIFF CONDITION
BY HERMAN WHITAKER

An Ontario sun shed a pleasant warmth into the clearing where Elder Hector McCakeron sat smoking. His gratified consciousness was pleasantly titillated by sights and sounds of worldly comfort. From the sty behind the house came fat gruntings; in the barn-yard hens were shrilly announcing that eggs would be served with the bacon; moreover, Janet was vigorously agitating a hoe among the potatoes to his left, while his wife performed similarly in the cabbage-garden. And what better could a man wish than to see his women profitably employed?

It was a pause in Janet's labors that gave the elder first warning of an intruder on his peace. A man was coming across the clearing--a short fellow, thick-set and bow-legged in figure, slow and heavy of face. The elder observed him with stony eyes.

"It's the Englisher," he muttered. "What'll he be wanting wi' me?"

His accent was hostile as his glance. Since, thirty years before, a wave of red-haired Scots inundated western Ontario, no man of Saxon birth had settled in Zorra, the elder's township. That in peculiar had been held sealed as a heritage to the Scot, and when Joshua Timmins bought out Sandy Cruikshanks the township boiled and burned throughout its length and breadth.

Not that it had expected to suffer the contamination. It was simply astounded at the man's impudence. "We'll soon drum him oot!" Elder McCakeron snorted, when he heard of the invasion; to which, on learning that Timmins was also guilty of Methodism, he added, "Wait till the meenister lays claws on the beast."

It was confidently expected that he would be made into a notable example, a warning to all intruders from beyond the pale; and the first Sunday after his arrival a full congregation turned out to see the minister do the trick. Interest was heightened by the presence of the victim, who, lacking a chapel of his own faith, attended kirk. His entrance caused a sensation. Forgetting its Sabbath manners, the congregation turned bodily and stared till recalled to its duty by the minister's cough. Then it shifted its gaze to him. What thunders were brewing behind that confident front? What lightnings lurked in the depths of those steel-gray eyes? Breathlessly Zorra had waited for the anathema which should wither the hardy intruder and drive him as chaff from a burning wind.

But it waited in vain. By the most liberal interpretation no phrase of his could be construed as a reflection on the stranger. Worse! After kirk-letting the minister hailed Timmins in the door, shook hands in the scandalized face of the congregation, and hoped that he might see him regularly at service.

Scandalous? It was irreligious! But if disappointed in its minister, Zorra had no intention of neglecting its own duty in the premises: the Englisher was not to be let off while memories of Bruce and Bannockburn lived in Scottish hearts. Which way he turned that day and in the months that followed he met dour faces. Excepting Cap'en Donald McKay, a retired mariner, whose native granite had been somewhat disintegrated by exposure to other climates, no man gave him a word;--this, of course, without counting Neil McNab, who called on Timmins three times a week to offer half-price for the farm.

With one exception, too, the women looked askance upon him, wondering, doubtless, how he dared to oppose their men-folks' wishes. Calling the cows of evenings, Janet McCakeron sometimes came on Timmins, whose farm cornered on her father's, and thus a nodding acquaintance arose between them. That she should have so demeaned herself is a matter of reproach with many, but the fair-minded who have sufficiently weighed the merits of her case are slower with their blames. For though Zorra can boast maidens who have hung in the wind till fifty and still, as the vernacular has it, "married on a man," a girl was counted well on the way to the shelf at forty-five. Janet, be it remembered, lacked but two years of the fatal age. Already chits of thirty-five or seven were generously alluding to her as the prop of her father's age; so small wonder if she simpered instead of passing with a nifty air when Timmins spoke one evening.

His remark was simple in tenor--in effect that her bell-cow was "a wee catham'ed"; but Janet scented its underlying tenderness as a hungry traveller noses a dinner on a wind, and after that drove her cows round by the corner which was conveniently veiled by heavy maple-bush. Indeed, it was to the friendly shadows which shrouded it, day or dark, that Cap'en McKay--a man wise in affairs of the heart by reason of much sailing in and out of foreign ports--afterward attributed the record which Timmins set Zorra in courting.

"He couldna see her bones, nor her his bow-legs," the mariner phrased it. But be this as it may, whether or no each made love to a voice, Cupid ran a swift course with them, steeplechasing over obstacles that would have taken years for a Zorra lad to plod around. In less than six months they passed from a bare goodnight to the exchange of soul thoughts on butter-making, the raising of calves, fattening of swine, and methods of feeding swedes that they might not taint cow's milk, and so had progressed by such tender paths through gentle dusks to the point where Timmins was ready to declare himself in the light of this present morning.

Assured by one glance that Timmins's courage still hung at the point to which she had screwed it the preceding evening, Janet drooped again to her work.

To his remark that the potatoes were looking fine, however, the elder made no response--unless a gout of tobacco smoke could be so counted. With eyes screwed up and mouth drawn down, he gazed off into space--a Highland sphinx, a Gaelic Rhadamanthus.

His manner, however, made no impression on Timmins's stolidity. The latter's eye followed the elder's in its peregrinations till it came to rest, when, without further preliminaries, he began to unfold his suit, which in matter and essence was such as are usually put forward by those whom love has blinded.

It was really an able plea, lacking perhaps those subtilities of detail with which a Zorra man would have trimmed it, but good enough for a man who labored under the disadvantages which accrue to birth south of the Tweed and Tyne. But it did not stir the elder's sphinxlike calm. "Ha' ye done?" he inquired, without removing his gaze from the clouds; and when Timmins assented, he delivered judgment in a cloud of tobacco smoke. "Weel--ye canna ha' her." After which he resumed his pipe and smoked placidly, wearing the air of one who has settled a difficult question forever.

But if stolid, Timmins had his fair share of a certain slow pugnacity.

"Why?" he demanded.

The elder smoked on.

"Why?"

"Weel,"--the elder spoke slowly to the clouds,--"I'm no obliged to quote chapter an' verse, but for the sake of argyment--forbye should Janet marry on an Englisher when there's good Scotchmen running loose?"

This was a "poser." Born to a full realization of the vast gulf which providence has fixed between the Highlands and the rest of the world, Janet recognized it as such. Pausing, she leaned on her hoe, anxiously waiting, while Timmins chewed a straw and the cud of reflection.

"Yes," he slowly answered, "they've been runnin' from 'er this twenty year." Nodding confirmation to the brilliant rejoinder, Janet fell again to work.

But the elder was in no wise discomposed. Withdrawing one eye from the clouds, he turned it approvingly upon her hoe practice. "She's young yet," he said, "an' a lass o' her pairts wull no go til the shelf."

"Call three-an'-forty young?"

"Christy McDonald," the elder sententiously replied, "marrit on Neil McNab at fifty. Janet's labor's no going to waste. An' if you were the on'y man i' Zorra, it wad behoove me to conseeder the lassie's prospects i' the next world. Ye're a Methodist."

"Meanin'," said Timmins, when his mind had grappled with the charge, "as there's no Methodists there?"

Questions of delicacy and certain theological difficulties involved called for reflection, and the elder smoked a full minute on the question before be replied: "No, I wadna go so far as that. It stan's to reason as there's some of 'em there; on'y--I'm no so sure o' their whereaboots."

Timmins thoughtfully scratched his head ere he came back to the charge. "Meanin' as there's none in 'eaven?"

Again the elder blew a reflective cloud over the merits of the question. "Weel," he said, delivering himself with slow caution, "if so--it's no on record."

Again Janet looked up, with defeat perching amid her freckles. "He's got ye this time," her face said, and the elder's expression of placid satisfaction affirmed the same opinion. But Timmins rose to a sudden inspiration.

"In 'eaven," he answered, "there's neither marriage nor givin' in marriage."

"Pish, mon!" the elder snorted. "It's no a question o' marrying; it's a question o' getting theer, an' Janet's no going to do it wi' a Methodist hanging til her skirts."

Silence fell in the clearing--silence that was broken only by the crash and tinkle of Janet's hoe as she buried Timmins under the clod. A Scotch daughter, she would bide by her father's word. Unaware of his funeral, Timmins himself stood scratching his poll.

"So you'll not give her to me?" he futilely repeated.

For the first time the elder looked toward him. "Mon, canna ye see the impossibility o' it? No, ye canna ha' her till--till"--he cast about for the limit of inconceivability--"till ye're an elder i' the Presbyterian Kirk." He almost cracked a laugh at Timmins's sudden brightening. He had evolved the condition to drive home and clinch the ridiculous impossibility of the other's suit, and here he was, the doddered fule, taking hope! It was difficult to comprehend the workings of such a mind, and though the elder smoked upon it for half an hour after Timmins left the clearing, he failed of realization.

"Yon's a gay fule," he said to Janet, when she answered his call to hitch the log farther into the cabin. "He was wanting to marry on you."

"Ay?" she indifferently returned,--adding, without change of feature, "There's no lack o' fules round here."

Meanwhile Timmins was making his way through the woods to his own place. As he walked along, the brightness gradually faded from his face, and by the time he reached the trysting-corner his mood was more in harmony with his case. His face would have graced a funeral.

Now Cap'en McKay's farm lay cheek by jowl with the elder's, and as the mariner happened to be fixing his fence at the corner, he noted Timmins's signals of distress. "Man!" he greeted, "ye're looking hipped." Then, alluding to a heifer of Timmins's which had **bloated** on marsh-grass the day before, he added, "The beastie didna die?" Assured that it was only a wife that Timmins lacked, he sighed relief. "Ah, weel, that's no so bad; they come cheaper. But tell us o't"

"Hecks, lad!" he commented, on Timmins's dole, "I'd advise ye to drive your pigs til anither market."

"Were?" Timmins asked--"w'ere'll I find one?"

"That's so." The mariner thoughtfully shaved his jaw with a red forefinger, while his comprehensive glance took in the other's bow-legs. "There isna anither lass i' Zorra that wad touch ye with a ten-foot pole."

Reddening, Timmins breathed hard, but the mariner met his stare with the serene gaze of one who deals in undiluted truth; so Timmins gulped and went on: "Say! I 'ear that you're mighty clever in these 'ere affairs. Can't you 'elp a feller out?"

The cap'en modestly bowed to reputation, admitting that he had assisted "a sight of couples over the broomstick," adding, however, that the knack had its drawbacks. There were many door-stones in Zorra that he dared not cross. And he wagged his head over Timmins's case, wisely, as a lawyer ponders over the acceptance of a hopeless brief. Finally he suggested that if Timmins was "no stuck on his Methodisticals," he might join the kirk.

"You think that would 'elp?"

The cap'en thought that, but he was not prepared to endorse Timmins's following generalization that it didn't much matter what name a man worshipped under. It penetrated down through the aforesaid rubble of disintegration and touched native granite. Stiffly enough he returned that Presbyterianism was good enough for him, but it rested on Timmins to follow the dictates of his own conscience.

Now when bathed in love's elixir conscience becomes very pliable indeed, and as the promptings of Timmins's inner self were all toward Janet, his outer man was not long in making up his mind. But though, following the cap'en's advice, he joined himself to the elect of Zorra, his change of faith brought him only a change of name.

Elder McCakeron officiated at the "christening" which took place in the crowded market the day after Timmins's name had been spread on the kirk register. "An' how is the apoos-tate the morning?" the elder inquired, meeting Timmins. And the name stuck, and he was no more known as the "Englisher."

"Any letters for the Apoos-tate?" The postmaster would mouth the question, repeating it after Timmins when he called for his mail. Small boys yelled the obnoxious title as he passed the log school on the corner; wee girls gazed after him, fascinated, as upon one destined for a headlong plunge into the lake of fire and brimstone. Summing the situation at the close of his second month's fellowship in the kirk, Timmins confessed to himself that it had brought him only a full realization of the "stiffness" of Elder McCakeron's "condition." He was no nearer to Janet, and never would have been but for the sudden decease of Elder Tammas Duncan.

In view of what followed, many hold that Elder Tammas made a vital mistake in dying, while a few, less charitable, maintain that his decease was positively sinful.

But if Elder Tammas be not held altogether blameless in the premises, what must be said of Saunders McClellan, who loaded himself with corn-juice and thereby sold himself to the fates? Saunders was a bachelor of fifty and a misogynist by repute. Twenty years back he had paid a compliment to Jean Ross, who afterward married on Rab Murray. It was not a flowery effort; simply to the effect that he, Saunders, would rather sit by her, Jean, than sup oatmeal brose. But though he did not soar into the realms of metaphor, the compliment seems to have been a strain on Saunders's intellect, to have sapped his being of tenderness; for after paying it he reached for his hat and fled, and never again placed himself in such jeopardy.

"Man!" he would exclaim, when, at threshing or logging bees, hairbreadth escapes from matrimony cropped up in the conversation,--"man! but I was near done for yon time!" And yet, all told, Saunders's dry bachelorhood seems to have been caused by an interruption in the flow rather than a drying up of his wells of feeling, as was proven by his conduct coming home from market the evening he overloaded with "corn-juice."

For as he drove by Elder McCakeron's milk-yard, which lay within easy hailing distance of the gravel road, Saunders bellowed to Janet: "Hoots, there! Come awa, my bonnie bride! Come awa to the meenister!" In front of her mother and Sib Sanderson, the cattle-buyer--who was pricing a fat cow,--Saunders thus committed himself, then drove on, chuckling over his own daring.

"Ye're a deevil! man, ye're a deevil!" he told himself, giving his hat a rakish cock. "Ye're a deevil wi' the weemen, a sair deceever."

He did feel that way--just then. But when, next morning, memory disentangled itself from a splitting headache, Saunders's red hair bristled at the thought of his indiscretion. It was terrible! He, Saunders, the despair of the girls for thirty years, had fallen into a pit of his own digging! He could but hope it a nightmare; but as doubt was more horrible than certainty, he dressed and walked down the line to

McCakeron's.

Once again he found Janet at the milking; or rather, she had just turned the cows into the pasture, and as she waited for him by the bars, Saunders thought he had never seen her at worse advantage. The sharp morning air had blued her nose, and he was dimly conscious that the color did not suit her freckles.

"Why, no!" she said, answering his question as to whether or no he had not acted a bit foolish the night before. "You just speired me to marry on you. Said I'd been in your eye this thirty years."

In a sense this was true. He had cleared from her path like a bolting rabbit, but gallantry forbade that manifest explanation. "'Twas the whuskey talking," he pleaded. "Ye'll no hold me til a drunken promise?"

But he saw, even before she spoke, that she would.

"'Deed but I will!" she exclaimed, tossing her head. "An' them says ye were drunken will ha' to deal wi' me. Ye were sober as a sermon."

Though disheartened, Saunders tried another tack. "Janet," he said, solemnly, "I dinna think as a well-brought lass like you wad care to marry on a man like me. I'm terrible i' the drink. I might beat ye."

Janet complacently surveyed an arm that was thick as a club from heavy choring. "I'll tak chances o' that."

Saunders's heart sank into his boots; but, wiping the sweat from his brow, he made one last desperate effort: "But ye're promised to the--the--Apoos-tate."

"I am no. Father broke that off."

Saunders shot his last bolt. "I believe I'm fickle, Janet. There'll be a sair heart for the lass that marries me. I wouldna wonder if I jilted ye."

"Then," she calmly replied, "I'll haul ye into the justice coort for breach o' promise."

With this terrible ultimatum dinging in his ears Saunders fled. Zorra juries were notoriously tender with the woman in the case, and he saw himself stripped of his worldly goods or tied to the apron of the homeliest girl in Zorra. One single ray illumined the dark prospect. That evening be called on Timmins, whom he much astonished by the extent and quality of his advice and encouragement. He even went so far as to invite the Englisher to his own cabin, thereby greatly scandalizing his housekeeper--a maiden sister of fifty-two, who had forestalled fate by declaring for the shelf at forty-nine.

"What'll he be doing here?" the maiden demanded, indicating Timmins with accusatory finger on the occasion of his first visit. But his meekness and the propitiatory manner in which he sat on the very edge of his chair, hat gripped between his knees, mollified her so much that she presently produced a bowl of red-cheeked apples for his refreshment.

But her thawing did not save Saunders after the guest was gone. "There's always a fule in every family," she cried, when he had explained his predicament, "an' you drained the pitcher."

"But you'll talk Janet to him," Saunders urged, "an' him to her? She's that hard put to it for a man that wi' a bit steering she'll consent to an eelopement."

But, bridling, Jeannie tossed a high head. "'Deed, then, an' I'll no do ither folk's love-making."

"Then," Saunders groaned, "I'll ha' the pair of ye in this hoose."

This uncomfortable truth gave Jeannie pause. The position of maiden sister carried with it more chores than easements, and Jeannie was not minded to relinquish her present powers. For a while she seriously studied the stove, then her face cleared; she started as one who suddenly sees her clear path, and giving Saunders a queer look, she said: "Ah, weel, you're my brother, after all. I'll do my best wi' both. Tell the Englisher as I'll be pleased to see him any time in the evening."

Matters were at this stage when Elder McCakeron's cows committed their dire trespass on Neil McNab's turnips.

Who would imagine that such unlike events as Saunders McClellan's lapse from sobriety, the death of Elder Duncan, and the trespass of McCakeron's cows could have any bearing upon one another? Yet from their concurrence was born the most astounding hap in the Zorra chronicles. Even if Elder McCakeron had paid Neil's bill of damage instead of remarking that he "didna see as the turnips had hurt his cows," the thing would have addled in the egg; and his recalcitrancy, so necessary to the hatching, has caused many a wise pow to shake over the inscrutability of Providence. But the elder did not pay, and in revenge Neil placed Peter Dunlop, the elder's ancient enemy, in nomination for Tammas Duncan's eldership.

It was Saunders McClellan who carried the news to the McCakeron homestead. According to her promise, Jeannie had visited early and late with Janet; and dropping in one evening to check up her report of progress, Saunders found the elder perched on a stump.

Saunders discharged him of his news, which dissipated the elder's calm as thunder shatters silence.

"What?" he roared. "Yon scunner? Imph! I'd as lief ... as lief ... elect"--the devil quivered back of his teeth, but as that savored of irreverence, he substituted "the Apoostate!"

Right here a devil entered in unto Saunders McClellan--the mocking devil whose mission it was to abase Zorra to the dust. But it did not make its presence known until, next day, Saunders carried the news of Elder McCakeron's retaliation to Cap'en McKay's pig-killing.

"He's going," Saunders informed the cap'en and Neil McNab between pigs,--"he's going to run Sandy 'Twenty-One' against your candidate."

Now between Neil and Sandy lay a feud which had its beginnings what time the latter *doctored* a spavined mare and sold her for a price to the former's cousin Rab.

"Yon scunner?" Neil exclaimed, using the very form of the elder's words, "yon scunner? I'd as lief ... as lief ... elect ..."

"... the Apoos-tate," said the Devil, though Neil thought that Saunders was talking.

"Ay, the Apoos-tate," he agreed.

"It wad be a fine joke," the Devil went on by the mouth of Saunders, "to run the Apoos-tate agin' his candidate. McCakeron canna thole the man."

"But what if he was elected?" the mariner objected.

The Devil was charged with glib argument. "We couldna very weel. It's to be a three-cornered fight, an' Robert Duncan, brother to Tammas, has it sure."

"'Twad be a good one on McCakeron," Neil mused. "To talk up Dunlop, who doesna care a cent for the eldership, an' then spring the Apoos-tate on him."

"'Twould be bitter on 'Twenty-One,'" the cap'en added. He had been diddled by Sandy on a deal of seed-wheat.

"It wad hit the pair of 'em," McNab chuckled, and with that word the Devil conquered.

So far, as aforesaid, Saunders had been unconscious of the Devil, but going home the latter revealed himself in a heart-to-heart talk. "Ye're no pretty to look at," Saunders said. "I'm minded to throw ye oot!"

The Devil chuckled. "Janet's so bonny. Fancy her on the pillow beside, ye--scraggy--bones--freckles. Hoots, man! a nightmare!"

Shuddering, Saunders reconsidered proceedings of ejectment. "But the thing is no posseeble?"

"You know your men," the Devil answered. "Close in the mouth as they are in the fist. McCakeron will never get wind o' the business till they spring it on him in meeting."

"That is so," Saunders acknowledged. "'Tis surely so-a."

"Then why," the Devil urged,--"then why not rig the same game on him?"

"Bosh! He wouldna think o't."

"Loving Dunlop as himself?" The Devil was apt at paraphrasing Scripture. "Imph!"

"It *would* let me out?" Saunders mused.

"Ye can but fail," argued the Devil. "Try it."

"I wull."

"This very night!" It is a wonder that the sparks did not fly, the Devil struck so hard on the hot iron. "To-night! Ye ken the election comes off next week."

"To-night," Saunders agreed.

Throughout that week the din of contending factions resounded beneath brazen harvest skies; for if there was a wink behind the clamor of any faction, it made no difference in the volume of its noise. Wherever two men foregathered, there the spirit of strife was in their midst; the burr of hot Scot's speech travelled like the murmur of robbed bees along the Side Lines, up the Concession roads, and even raised an echo in the hallowed seclusion of the minister's study. And harking back to certain eldership elections in which the breaking of heads had taken the place of "anointing with oil," Elder McIntosh quietly evolved a plan whereby the turmoil should be left outside the kirk on election night.

But while it lasted no voice rang louder than that of Saunders McClellan's devil. Not a bit particular in choice of candidates, he roared against Dunlop, Duncan, or "Twenty-One" according to the company which Saunders kept. "Ye havna the ghaist of a show!" he assured Cap'en McKay, chief of the Dunlopers. "McCakeron

drew three mair to him last night." While to the elder he exclaimed the same day:
"Yon crazy sailorman's got all the Duncanites o' the run. He has ye spanked, Elder.
Scunner the deil!" So the Devil blew, hot and cold, with Saunders's mouth, until the
very night before the election.

The morning of the election the sun heaved up on a brassy sky. It was intensely
hot through the day, but towards evening gray clouds scudded out of the east, veil-
ing the sun with their twisting masses; at twilight heavy rain-blots were splashing
the dust. At eight o'clock, meeting-time, rain flew in glistening sheets against the
kirk windows and forced its way under the floor. There was but a scant attendance--
twoscore men, perhaps, and half a dozen women, who sat, in decent Scotch fashion,
apart from the men--that is, apart from all but Joshua Timmins. Not having been
raised in the decencies as observed in Zorra, he had drifted over to the woman's side
and sat with Janet McCakeron and Jean McClellan, one on either side.

But if few in number, the gathering was decidedly formidable in appearance.
As the rain had weeded out the feeble, infirm, and pacifically inclined, it was distinctly belligerent in character. Grim, dour, silent, it waited for the beginning of
hostilities.

Nor did the service of praise which preceded the election induce a milder spirit. When the precentor led off, "Howl, ye Sinners, Howl! Let the Heathen Rage and
Cry!" each man's look told that he knew well whom the psalmist was hitting at;
and when the minister invoked the "blind, stubborn, and stony-hearted" to "depart
from the midst," one-half of his hearers looked their astonishment that the other
half did not immediately step out in the rain. A heavy inspiration, a hard sigh, told
that all were bracing for battle when the minister stepped down from the pulpit,
and noting it, he congratulated himself on his precautions against disturbance.

"For greater convenience in voting," he said, reaching paper slips and a box of
pencils from behind the communion rail, "we will depart from the oral method and
elect by written ballot"

He had expected a protest against such a radical departure from ancestral prec-
edent, but in some mysterious way the innovation seemed to jibe with the people's
inclination.

"Saunders McClellan," the minister went on, "will distribute and collect ballot-
ing-papers on the other aisle."

"Give it to him, Cap'en!" Saunders whispered, as he handed him a slip. "He's glowering at ye."

The elder was indeed surveying the mariner, McNab, and Dunlop with a glance of comprehensive hostility over the top of his ballot. "See what I'm aboot!" his look said, as he folded the paper and tossed it into Saunders's hat.

"The auld deevil!" McNab whispered, as the minister unfolded the first ballot. "He'll soon slacken his gills."

"That'll be one of oor ballots," the cap'en hoarsely confided.

The minister was vigorously rubbing his glasses for a second perusal of the ballot, but when the third, fourth, fifth, and sixth were added to the first, his face became a study in astonishment. And presently his surprise was reflected by the congregation. For whereas three candidates were in nomination, the ballots were forming but two piles.

Whispers ran through the kirk; the cap'en nudged McNab.

"McCakeron must ha' swung all the Duncanites?"

"Ah," Neil muttered. "An' that wad account for the stiff look o' the reptile. See the glare o't."

They would have stiffened in astonishment could they have translated the "glare." "Got the Duncanites, did ye?" the elder was thinking. "Bide a wee, bide a wee! He laughs best that laughs last."

Saunders McClellan and his Devil alone sensed the inwardness of those two piles, and they held modest communion over it in the back of the kirk. "You may be ugly, but ye've served me well," Saunders began.

The Devil answered with extreme politeness: "You are welcome to all ye get through me. If no honored, ye are at least aboot to become famous in your ain country."

"Infamous, I doobt, ye mean," Saunders corrected. Then, glancing uneasily toward the door, he added, "I think as we'd better be leaving."

"Pish!" the Devil snorted. "They are undone by their ain malignancy. See it oot."

"That's so," Saunders agreed. "That is surely so-a. Hist! The meenister's risen. Man, but he's tickled to death over the result. His face is fair shining."

The minister did indeed look pleased. Stepping down to the floor that he might be closer to these his people, he beamed benevolently upon them while he made a little speech. "People of Scottish birth," he said, closing, "are often accused of being hard and uncharitable to the stranger in their gates, but this can never be said of you who have extended the highest honor in your gift to a stranger; who have elected Brother Joshua Timmins elder in your kirk by a two-thirds majority."

The benediction dissolved the paralysis which held all but Saunders McClellan; but stupefaction remained. Astounding crises are generally attended with little fuss, from the inability of the human intellect to grasp their enormous significance. As John "Death" McKay afterward put it, "Man, 'twas so extraordin'ry as to seem ordin'ry." Of course neither Dunlopers nor "Twenty-One's" were in a position to challenge the election, and if the Duncanites growled as they pawed over the ballots, their grumbling was presently silenced by a greater astonishment.

For out of such evenings history is made. While the minister had held forth on the rights and duties of eldership, Saunders McClellan's gaze had wandered over to Margaret McDonald--a healthy, red-cheeked girl--and he had done a little moralizing on his own account. In the presence of such an enterprising spinsterhood, bachelorhood had become an exceedingly hazardous existence, and if a man must marry, be might as weel ha' something young an' fresh! Margaret, too, was reputed industrious as pretty! Of Janet's decision, Saunders had no doubts. Between himself and Jeannie, and Timmins--meek, mild, and unencumbered--there could be no choice. Still there was nothing like certainty; 'twas always best to be off wi' the old, an' so forth!

Rising, he headed for Janet, who, with her father, Jeannie, Timmins, and the minister, stood talking at the vestry door. As he made his way forward, he reaped a portion of the Devil's promised fame. As they filed sheepishly down the aisle, the Dunlopers gave him the cold shoulder, and when he joined the group, Elder Mc-Cakeron returned a stony stare to his greeting.

"But ye needna mind that," the Devil encouraged. "He daurna tell, for his own share i' the business."

So Saunders brazened it out. "Ye ha' my congratulations, Mr. McCakeron. I hear you're to get a son-in-law oot o' this?"

If Elder McCakeron had given Saunders the tempter the glare which he now bestowed on Saunders the successfully wicked, he had not been in such lamentable case.

"Why, what is this?" the minister exclaimed. "Cause for further congratulation, Brother Timmins?"

Saunders now shone as Cupid's assistant. "He was to ha' Janet on condeetion that he made the eldership," he fulsomely explained.

The minister's glance questioned the elder.

"Well," he growled, "I'm no going back on my word."

Saunders glowed all over, and in exuberance of spirit actually winked at Margaret McDonald across the kirk. Man, but she was pretty!

"It's to your credit, Mr. McCakeron, that you should hold til a promise," Jeannie was saying. "But ye'll no be held. A man may change his mind, and since you refused Joshua, he's decided to marry on me."

Saunders blenched. He half turned to flee, but Janet's strong fingers closed on his sleeve; and as her lips moved to claim him before minister and meeting, he thought that he heard the Devil chuckling, a great way off.

IN THE INTERESTS OF CHRISTOPHER
BY MAY HARRIS

Mrs. Manstey's big country-house was temporarily empty of the guests she had gathered for a week-end in June when the two Eversley girls reached it, Saturday at noon. Their hostess met them at the door when the carriage wheels crunched on the gravelled curve of the drive before the house--a charming gray-haired woman of sixty, with a youthful face and a delicate girlish color.

"I've sent everybody away to explore--to ravage the country," she gayly explained the emptiness of the large hall, where the grouped chairs seemed recently vacated and pleasantly suggestive of suspended tete-a-tete. "I've had Rose before," Mrs. Manstey pursued, taking them up the stairs to their rooms, "but not *you!*" She gave Edith's shoulder an affectionate little pat. She thought the younger girl extremely beautiful--which she was, with a vivid, piquant face and charming eyes.

"I've had my day," Rose Eversley acknowledged, with her usual air of jesting gravity, that, almost ironic, made one always a little unsure of her. "Dear Mrs. Manstey, you perfectly see--don't you?--that Edith is papa's image, and--"

"And he was my old sweetheart!" Mrs. Manstey completed, with humorous appreciation of her own repetition of an old story.

"Was he, really?" Edith wondered. "Mamma says you were *her* friend."

Mrs. Manstey laughed. "Couldn't I have been--both?" she gayly put it. "Friends are better than sweethearts--they last longer. Though of course you won't agree, at your age, to such heresy."

"Sweethearts?" the girl pondered as she lifted her hands to take off her hat. "I--don't know. It's such a pretty word, but it doesn't mean much these days--there aren't any!" She shrugged her shoulders with a petulant pessimism her youth made amusing. "Papa was the last of the kind--he's a *love!*--and you let mamma have him!"

"I didn't 'let.'" Mrs. Manstey enjoyed it. "When he met your mother he forgot all about me. Think of it! I haven't seen either him or your mother in years, years, years!"

"My years!" Edith said. "I was a baby, mamma says, when she saw you last."

"So you were."

A servant knocked, with a note for Mrs. Manstey. As she took it and turned to leave the room, her smile, caressingly including Rose, went past her and lingered a thought longer--as people's smiles had a way of doing--with Edith.

"I know you're tired," she added to her smile. "Five hours of train--Get into something cool and rest. Luncheon isn't until two."

She disappeared, and Rose looked at her sister, who, with her hat in her hand, was going into her room.

"Well--?" Rose lifted her voice in its faint drawl of interrogation.

Edith looked at her absently. "I don't know," she said, drawing her straight brows into a puzzled frown. "I'm as far away as ever--I'm so perplexed."

"Well--you'll *have* to decide, you know."

Edith shook her head impatiently and went into her room, closing the door. She hurried out of her dusty travelling things into cool freshness, and, settled in the most comfortable chair, gave herself up to an apparently endless fit of musing. She was so physically content that her mind refused to respond with any vigorous effort; to think at all was a crumpled rose-leaf.

From the lower hall the clock chimed one with musical vibrations. Edith leaned forward with her chin on her hand, driving her thoughts into a definite path. The curtains stirred in a breeze from the out-of-doors whose domain swept with country greenness and adventitious care away from the window under the high brilliance of the sun.

Close to the window a writing-table, with blotter, pens, and ink, made a focal-point for her gaze. At first a mere detail in her line of vision, it attained by degrees, it seemed, a definite relevancy to her train of thought. She looked in her portmanteau for her desk, and getting out some note-paper, went to the table and began to write a letter.

What she had to say seemed difficult to decide. She wrote a line, stared out of the window with fixity, and then wrote again--a flurry of quick, decisive strokes as if at determinate pressure. But a sigh struck across her mood, and almost against her will the puzzled crinkle returned to her brow. The curtain blew against her face, disarranging her hair, and as she lifted her hand to put back a straggling lock, the wind tossed the sheet of the letter she was writing out of the window. Her eyes, as she sprang up, followed its flight, but it whirled around the corner of the house and was lost to her desperate gaze.

Neglige, even of the most-becoming description, was not to be thought of in pursuing the loss, for the silence of the house had stirred to the sound of gay voices, the movement of feet.

Rose, also in neglige, opened the door between them and found her madly tearing off her pale-blue kimono. "What's the matter?" She paused, staring.

"Heavens! My shoes--please!--there by the table." She kicked off her ridiculous blue slippers and pulled on the small colonials her sister in open wonder handed her. "If you had only been dressed," she almost wailed, "you might have been able to get it."

"Get what?"

"My letter!" Tragic, in spite of a mouthful of pins--which is a woman's undoubted preference, no matter how many befrilled pincushions entreat a division of spoils,--she turned her face with its import of sudden things to her sister in explanation. "I was writing a letter and it blew out of the window!"

"Well, if it did--"

"But, don't you see?--I was writing to **Christopher!** I had been thinking and thinking, and at last I screwed up my courage to answer his letter. I had all but signed my name!"

Rose Eversley began to laugh helplessly; heartlessly, her sister thought.

"If you hadn't signed it--" she at last comforted her sister's indignant face that was reflected from the mirror, where she stood as she fastened the white stock at her throat and snapped the clasp of her belt.

"Signed it!" She was almost in tears. "What difference will that make when I claim the letter? I *must* find it! But of course some one who knows me will be sure to find it. And *that* letter, of all letters!"

"If I were you, Edith," Rose advised, calmly, "I shouldn't--"

"Well?"--with her hand on the door-knob.

"--try to find it. It will be impossible to trace it to you, in that case."

"But *don't* you see--"

"Wait!" Rose caught and pulled her back. "How *could* they know? You'll get in much deeper. What had you written?"

"I said, 'Dear Christopher'--"

Rose laughed. "I'm glad you didn't say 'Dear Mr. Brander.' In that case you'd have given *him* away. But 'Christopher' is such an unusual name, they might-- Sherlock Holmes could trace him by it alone."

"You *are* a Job's comforter--a perfect Eliphaz the Temanite! Oh, oh!" Her soft crescendo was again tragic.

"In effect you said: 'Dear Christopher, as you have so often entreated, I have at last decided to be thine. The tinkle of thy shekels, now that I am so nearly shekel-less myself, has done its fatal worst. I am thine--'"

"Oh, let me go!" Edith cried, in a fury close to tears. "You haven't any feeling. You are not going to sacrifice *your*self!"

"To a good-looking young man who loves me exceedingly, and to something over a million? No, I am not!" Rose said, dryly.

"Oh, it's dreadful! Perfectly!" Edith cried, and on her indecision Rose hung another bit of wisdom:

"Why don't you go down in a leisurely way and investigate? You know the direction it blew away; follow it. If you meet any one, be admiring the scenery!"

Again Edith's look deserved the foot-lights, but Rose shrugged her shoulders and withdrew her detaining hand. Edith caught up her parasol and ran down the stairs. The big hall was empty. From a room on the right came a click of billiard-balls.

"Perhaps they are all in the house!" she thought, and drew a small breath of relief.

On the door-step she paused, with her parasol open, and considered. The house faced the west; her room was to the south, and the letter had disappeared to the east. She chose her line of advance carefully careless.

The lawn on the eastern side of the house sloped to an artificial pond, and near it a vine-covered summer-house made a dim retreat from the June sun. Look as she would, though, no faintest glimpse of white paper rewarded her gaze.

She strolled on--daunted, but still persistent, with the wind blowing her hair out of order--to the door of the summer-house. Within it a young man was standing, reading her letter. He looked up and took off his hat hastily, crumpling the letter in his hand. She saw he was quite ugly, with determined-looking eyes, and the redemption of a pleasant mouth.

She hesitated, the words "That is my letter!" absolutely frozen on her lips. He had been reading it! It seemed impossible for her to claim it, and so for a moment's silence she stood, with the green vines of the doorway--

Half light, half shade--

framing herself and her white umbrella.

"You are looking for a cool spot?"--he deprecatingly took the initiative. "This is a good choice. There's a wind--"

"Horrid!" she interrupted, so vehemently that she caught his involuntary surprise. "I don't like the wind," she added.

"'It's an ill wind,' you know, 'that doesn't blow some one good.'"

"I assure you *this* is an ill wind! It has blown me all of the ill it could."

"Do come out of it," he begged. "The vines keep it off. It's a half-hour until luncheon," he added, "unless they've changed since I was here last." He put up his watch. "We're fellow guests. You came this morning, didn't you?--while we were out. I came last night."

She seated herself provisionally on the little bench by the door, and dug the point of her umbrella into the ground. Her mind was busy. He still held the letter. She had had a forlorn hope that he would throw down the sheet; but he did not. Was there any strategy, she wondered. But none suggested itself; and indeed, as if divining her thought, he put the crumpled sheet in his pocket. Her eyes followed despairingly the "Dear Christopher," in her clear and, she felt, unfortunately individual writing, as it disappeared in his capacious blue serge pocket.

Different ideas wildly presented themselves, but none would do. Could she ask him to climb a tree? Of course in that case he would have to take off his coat and put it down, and give her the opportunity to recover the horrible letter from his pocket. But one cannot ask a stranger to climb a tree simply to exhibit his acrobatic powers. And trees!--there were none save saplings in a radius of fifty yards! Could she tumble in the pond? It would be even less desirable, and he would simply wade in and pull her out, with no need to remove his coat.

"Mrs. Manstey," he was saying, a little tentatively, upholding the burden of conversation, "sent some of us out riding this morning, and Ralph Manstey raced us home by a short cut cross country. That is, he took the short cut. *We* gave it the cut direct and looked for gaps."

"If I had been out, I'd have taken every fence," she said, boastfully, and then laughed. He laughed too.

"If I--if you were my sister, I shouldn't let you follow Ralph Manstey on horseback. He's utterly reckless."

"So am I," she came in, with spirit. "At home I ride anything and jump everything."

"Well, you shouldn't if you were my sister," he repeated, decisively.

"I'm sorry for your sister," she declared.

"Well, you see, I haven't one," he said, gayly, and smiled down at her lifted face. Remembering the letter, she corrected her expression to colder lines.

"There's no one to introduce us,"--he broke the pause. "Mayn't I--" He colored and put his hand into his pocket, and taking out her letter, folded the blank sheet out and produced a pencil. "It's hard to call one's own name," he continued. "Suppose we write our names?"

As he was clumsy in finesse, she understood his idea, and her eyes flashed. But she said nothing as he scribbled and handed the paper to her. She read, "C.K. Farringdon," and played with the pencil.

"Mr. Farringdon,"--she said it over meditatively. "How plainly you write! My name's Edith Eversley," she added, tranquilly, and, because she must, per force, returned the sheet to him. She had a wicked delight in the defeat of his strategy which she could cleverly conceal.

"I wish," he deprecated, gently, but with persistence, "that you would write your name here--won't you, as a souvenir?"

But she shook her head and rose--angry, which she hid, but also amused at his pertinacity.

"I can't write decently with a pencil," she said, carelessly, and her eyes followed his hand putting the letter back into his pocket. That she should have actually had the letter in her hand, and had to give it back! But no quick-witted pretext had occurred to help her. Rose would think her stupid--utterly lacking in expedients.

She left the summer-house, unfurling her umbrella, and Farringdon followed instantly, his failure apparently forgotten.

They passed the tennis-court on their way to the house, and--

"Do you play?" he asked.

"A little." Her intonation mocked the formula.

"Might we, then, this afternoon--"

She gave him a side glance. "If you don't mind losing," she suggested.

"But I play to win," he modestly met it, and again they laughed.

Rose Eversley looked with curiosity at her sister when she entered the dining-room for luncheon, followed by Farringdon, but Edith's face was non-committal. She was bright and vivacious, and made herself very pleasant to Farringdon, who sat by her. After luncheon they went to the tennis-court together.

"A delightful young man," Mrs. St. Cleve commented, putting up her lorgnette as she stood at the window with Rose, watching their disappearing figures, "but so far as money is concerned, a hopeless detrimental. Don't let your pretty sister get interested in him. He hasn't a cent except what he makes--he's an architect."

"Edith is to be depended upon," Rose said, enigmatically. She was five years older than her sister, and had drawn the inference of her own plainness, comparatively, ever since Edith had put on long dresses.

"Have you written to Christopher?" she asked, that night, invading Edith's room with her hair-brushes.

"No, I haven't," Edith said, thoughtfully. "I tried just now. It seems--I don't know how, exactly, but I just *can't* write it over again! If I had the letter I wrote this morning, I suppose I would send it; but to write it all over again--it's too horrible!"

"'Horrible'!" Rose repeated. "Very few people would think it that! He's rich, thoroughly good, and devoted to you."

"You put the least last," Edith said, slowly, "and you're right. I'm not sure Christopher is so devoted to me, after all. He may only fancy that I like him, and from his high estate--"

"Nonsense!" Rose said, warmly. "He isn't, as you know, that sort of a man. I've known him for years--" She paused.

Edith said nothing; she brushed her hair with careful slowness.

"He is so sincere--so straight-forward," Rose went on, in an impersonal tone; "and as papa has had so much ill luck and our circumstances have changed--they *are* changed, you know, though we are still able to keep up a certain appearance--he has been unchanged. You ought to consider--"

"You consider Christopher's interests altogether," Edith said. "I've some, too."

"Oh no! You needn't think of them with Christopher," Rose said, seriously. "That's just it! He would so completely look after *yours!* It's *his*, in this regard, that need consideration."

"Well--I'll consider Christopher's interests," Edith said, quietly.

She remembered perfectly the letter she had written--which was in an ugly young man's pocket! It had been

"DEAR CHRISTOPHER,--Do you think you really want me? If you are very sure, I am willing. I don't care for anybody else, so perhaps I can learn to care for you.

"The only thing is, you will spoil me, and they've done that at home already! and Rose says I need a strong hand! So in your interests--" and then it had blown away!

When Rose, after some desultory talk, went back to her room, Edith wrote another letter:

"DEAR CHRISTOPHER,--I know you have made a mistake. I don't care for you--to marry you--a bit, but I like you, oh, a quantity! We have always been such friends, and we always will be, won't we? but not *that* way.

"Some day you will be very happy with some one else who will suit you better. Then you will know how right I am.

With kindest wishes,
EDITH EVERSLEY."

She took this letter down the next morning to put in the bag, but the postman had come and gone. As she stood in the hall holding the letter, Farringdon came up.

"Good morning," he said. "You've missed the postman? I will be very happy to post it for you on my way to church."

"Thank you. But if it's on the way to church, I'm going myself, so I needn't trouble you."

Farringdon merely bowed, without saying anything banal about the absence of trouble. She was demurely conscious beneath his courtesy of the effort he was making to see her handwriting, and she wondered if he thought her refusal rude and a confirmation of his suspicion, or simply casual.

Whatever he thought, it did not prevent the steps as she came out a few hours later in the freshness of white muslin, with her umbrella, prayer-book, and an unobtrusive white envelope in her hands.

They were going together down then drive--under his umbrella--before she quite grasped the situation.

"We seem to be the only ones," she hazarded.

"We are," he nodded.

"Mrs. Manstey has a headache," Edith said, "but the others--"

"The sun is too hot!"--he smiled.

"But you--I shouldn't have thought--" She paused, a little embarrassed.

"Yes?" he helped her. "That I was one of those who go to church, you mean?"

"Oh no!" she protested; but it was what she had meant.

"You are right," he said, without heeding the protest, and his ugly but compellingly attractive face was turned to hers. "I'm not in the least a scoffer, though; pray believe that. It's just that I--" he hesitated. "Do you remember a little verse:

'Although I enter not,
Yet round about the spot
Sometimes I hover,
And at the sacred gate
With longing eyes I wait,
Expectant of her.'"

Her face flushed. "But," she reverted, with naivete, "you said you were going to church--"

"But because I knew you were one of the women who would be sure to go!" he said, positively.

She rebelled. "I don't look devotional at all!"

"But your eyes do," he declared. "They're suggestive of cathedrals and beautiful dimness, and a voice going up and up, like the 'Lark' song of Schubert's, don't you know!"

"No, I ***don't!***" she said, wilfully; but she was conscious of his eyes on her face, and angry that her cheeks flushed.

They both were silent for a little, and when they left Mrs. Manstey's grounds for the uneven country road, that became shortly, by courtesy, the village street, they had a view of the little church with its tiny tower.

"The post-office," Farringdon explained, "is at the other end of the street. Service is beginning, I dare say. Shall we wait until it is over, or post the letter now?"

"No; after service," she agreed, and inopportunely the letter slipped from her hand and fell, with the address down, on the grass. She stooped hurriedly, but he was before her, and picking it up, returned it scrupulously, with the right side down, as it had fallen. She slipped it quickly, almost guiltily, into her prayer-book.

The church was small, the congregation smaller, and the clergyman a little weary of the empty benches. But the two faces in the Manstey pew were so bright, so vivid with the vigor of youth, that his jaded mind freshened to meet the interest of new hearers.

But neither Edith nor Farringdon listened attentively to the sermon, for their minds were busy with other things. He was thinking of the girl beside him, whose hymnal he was sharing, and whose voice, very sweet and clear, if of no great compass, blended with his own fine tenor. Her thoughts could not stray far from the letter and--from other things!

The benediction sent them from the cool dimness into the sunlight, and she looked down the street toward the post-office.

"It's quite at the other end of the street," Farringdon said, opening his umbrella and tentatively discouraging the effort. "By the way, your letter won't leave, I remember, until the seven-o'clock train. The Brathwaites are leaving by that train; you can send your letter down then."

She found herself accepting this proposition, for the blaze of the sun on the length of the dusty street was deterring. They walked back almost in silence the way they had come; but with his hand on Mrs. Manstey's gate and the house less than two hundred yards away, Farringdon paused.

"You have been writing to 'Christopher,'" he said, quietly. "I don't want you to send the letter." He was quite pale, but she did not notice it or the tensity of his face; his audacity made her for the moment dumb.

"You don't want me to--!" She positively gasped. "I never heard of such--"

"Impertinence," he supplied, gravely. "It looks that way, I know, but it isn't. I can't stand on conventions--I've too much at stake. I don't mean to lose *you*--as you lost your letter!"

She thought she was furious. "You knew it was my letter!" she accused.

They had paused just within the gate, in the shade of a great mulberry-tree that stood sentinel.

"Forgive me," he said. "Not at first--but I guessed it. My name," he added, "is Christopher, too."

He took a crumpled sheet, that had been smoothed and folded carefully, from his pocket. "Do you remember what you wrote?" he asked, in a low voice.

Her face was crimson.

"It blew to me. Such things don't happen every day." He had taken off his hat, and, bareheaded, he bent and looked questioningly into her eyes. "My name is Christopher," he repeated. "I can't--it isn't possible--that I can let another Christopher have that letter."

Her eyes fell before his.

"I"--he paused--"I play tennis very well, you said. I play to win! What I give to the interest of a game--"

"Is nothing to what you give to the interests of Christopher!"

As she mockingly spoke, Farringdon caught a glimpse of one or two people strolling down from the house. "That letter," he hastily said,--"you can't take it from me! Do you remember that wind? It blew *you* to *me!* Dearest, *darling*, don't be angry. You *can't* take yourself away."

A little smile touched her lips--mutinous, but tremulous, too, and something in her look made his heart beat fast.

"I didn't--The last letter wasn't like the first," she said, incoherently, but it seemed he understood.

"I knew you were *you* as soon as I saw you," he said, idiotically.

"And," she murmured, as they walked perforce to meet the people coming toward them down the drive, "after all, you *were* Christopher!"

THE WRONG DOOR
BY FRANCIS WILLING WHARTON

The stairs were long and dark; they seemed to stretch an interminable length, and she was too tired to notice the soft carpet and wonder why Mrs. Wilson had departed from her iron-clad rules and for once considered the comfort of her lodgers. The rail of the banisters lay cold but supporting under the pressure of her weary hand, and, at her own door at last, she fitted the key in the lock. Something was wrong; it would not turn; she drew it out and tried the handle. The door opened, and entering, she stood rooted to the spot.

Had her poor little room doubled its size and trebled its furniture? Her imagination, always active, for one wild moment suggested that old Grandaunt Crosbie from over the seas had remembered her poor relatives and worked the miracle; she always had Grandaunt Crosbie as a possible trump in the hand of fate. And then the dull reality shattered her foolish castle--she was in the wrong room. All this comfort had a legitimate possessor, whose Aunt Crosbie did her proper part in life.

She walked mechanically to a window and looked down; yes, there was the bleak yard she usually found below her, four houses off; she had come into the wrong door, and now to retrace her useless steps.

She paused a moment, and slowly revolving, made bitter inventory of the charming interior. Soft, bright stuffs at the windows, on the chairs; pictures; books; flowers even; a big bunch of holly on the mantelpiece. A sitting-room--no obnoxious bed behind an inadequate screen, no horrid white china pitcher in full view! What woman owned all this? She stared about for characteristic traces. No sewing! Pipes! It belonged to a man.

She must go. She moved toward the door, and dropped her eyes on the little hard-coal fire in the grate; it tempted her, and, with a sort of defiance, she moved over to it and warmed her chilled fingers. A piano, too, and not to teach children on! To play upon, to enjoy! When was her time to come? Every dog has his day! Where was hers? Here some man was surrounded with comforts and pleasures, and she slaved all day at her teaching, and came home at night tired, cold, to a miserable little half-furnished room--alone.

Resting her arms on the mantelpiece, she dropped her face a moment on them and rebelled, kicking hard against the pricks; and sunk in that profitless occupation, heard vaguely the sound of rapid steps and suddenly realized what they might mean.

She straightened her young form and stared, fascinated, at the door. Good heavens! What should she do? What should she say? If she appeared confused, she would be thought a thief; she must have some excuse: she had come--to--find a lady--was waiting! She sank into a little chair and tried not to tremble visibly to the most unobservant eye, and the door opened, shut, and the owner of the room stood before her.

"How do you do?" said Amory, and coming forward, he shook hands warmly. "Please forgive me for being late, but I could not get away a moment before. Where" he looked about the room--"where is Mrs. White?"

The girl had risen nervously, and stood with her fingers clasped, looking at him; she answered, stammering, "She--I--she--couldn't come."

"Couldn't come?" repeated the young man. "I'm awfully sorry. Do sit down."

She still stood, holding to the back of her chair. "She said she would come if she could, and I was to--but I had better go."

Amory laughed. "Not a bit of it. Now I've got you, I sha'n't let you go. It was very brave of you to come alone. You know brothers-in-law are presumptuous sometimes." He smiled down into the soft, shy, dark eyes raised to his, and looked at his watch. "You must have waited a half-hour; I said four o'clock. I'm so sorry."

Her eyes dropped. "I was late, too," she answered, and felt a horrible weight lifted from her. (They surely could not be coming; she could go in a moment; he would never know until she was beyond his reach. But she reckoned without her host.)

"Draw up to the fire," he began, and wheeled up a big armchair, and gently made her sit in it. "Put your feet on the fender and let's have a long talk. You know

I sha'n't see you before the wedding, and I'd like to know something of my brother's wife. Tom said I must see you once before you and he got off to Paris, and I may not be able to get West for the wedding; so this is the one chance I shall have." He drew his chair near, and looked down at her with friendly, pleasant eyes.

She must say something. She rested her head on the high back of her chair, and felt a sensation of bewildered happiness. It was dangerous; she must get away in a moment; but for a moment she might surely enjoy this extraordinary situation that fortune had thrust upon her--the charm of the room, the warmth, and something more wonderful still--companionship. She looked at him; she must say something.

"You think you can't come to the wedding?" she said, and blushed.

Amory shook his head. "I'm afraid not, though of course I shall try. Now"--he stared gravely at her--"now tell me how you came to know Tom and why you like him. I wonder if it is for my reasons or ones of your own."

He was surprised by the deep blush which answered his words. What a wonderful wild-rose color on her rather pale cheek!

"Don't you think it very warm in here?" said the girl.

Amory got up, and going to the window, opened it a little; then, stopping at his desk, picked up a note and brought it to the fire.

"Why, here is a note from Mrs. White," he said. "Why didn't you tell me?"

She had risen, and laid her hand an instant on his arm. "Don't open it--yet," she said. Her desperation lent her invention; just in this one way he must not find her out. She gave him a look, half arch, half pleading. "I'll explain later," she said.

Amory felt a stir of most unnecessary emotion; he understood Tom.

"Of course," he said, dropping it on the mantelpiece,--"just as you like. Now let's go back to Tom. You see,"--he sat down, and tipping his chair a little, gave her a rather curious smile,--"Tom and I have been enigmas to each other always, deeply attached and hopelessly incomprehensible, and I had my own ideas of what Tom would marry--and--you are not it;--not in the least!" He leant forward and brought his puzzled gaze to bear upon her.

She settled deeply into her chair, half to get farther away from those searching gray eyes, half because she was taking terrible risks, and she might as well enjoy it; the chair was so comfortable, and the fire so cheerful, and Amory--it occurred to her with a sort of exhilaration what it would be to please him. She had pleased other people, why not him? Her lids drooped; she looked down at her shabby gloves.

"What did you expect?" she said.

He leant back and laughed. "What did I expect? Well, frankly, a silly little blond thing, all curls and furbelows!"

She raised those heavy lids of hers and gazed straight at him. "Was that Tom's description?" she asked, and raised her eyebrows. They were delicately pencilled, and Amory watched her and noted them.

"No," he answered; "he didn't describe you, but I thought that was his taste. Now, you are neither silly nor little; no blonde; you have no curls and no furbelows. In fact"--he smiled with something delightfully intimate in his eyes--"in fact, you are much more the kind of girl *I* should like to marry."

It gave her an absurd little thrill. She sat up, rebellious. "If *I* would have liked you," she returned.

Amory laughed and put his hands in his pockets. "Of course," he said; "but you would, you know!"

"Why?" she demanded, opening her eyes very wide; and again he inwardly complimented her on her eyebrows, and above them her hair grew in a charming line on her forehead. The little points are all pretty, he thought, and it is the details that count in the long run. How much one could grow to dislike blurry eyebrows and ugly ears, even if a woman had rosy cheeks and golden hair!

"Why? Because I should bully you into it. I'm an obstinate kind of creature, and get things by hanging on. Women give in if you worry them long enough. But tell me more about Tom," he went on. "Did he dance and shoot his way into your heart? I wish I'd been there to see! You take a very bad tintype, by the way. Tom sent me that." He got up, and taking a picture from the mantelpiece, tossed it into her lap, and leaning over the back of her chair, looked down on it. "Have you a sentiment about it?" he added, smiling. "It does look like Tom."

She held it and gravely studied it. She colored, and, still looking at the picture, felt her way suddenly open. "Yes, it does look like him," she said, and putting it down, leant forward and looked into the fire. "Do you want to know why I accepted Tom?" she added, slowly. She was fully launched on a career of deception now, and felt a desperate exultation.

Amory stared at her and nodded.

She kept her eyes on the fire. "I wanted--a home."

Amory sat motionless, then spoke. "Why--why, weren't you happy with your aunt and uncle?"

She shook her head. "No; and Tom was good and kind and very--"

Amory got up and shook himself. "Oh, but that's an awful mistake," he said.

"I know," said the girl, and turning, looked at him a moment. "Well, I've come to tell you that I have--" She hesitated.

Amory slid down into the chair beside her. "Changed your mind?"

"Yes."

"That note of your aunt's?"

"Yes"

He sat back and folded his arms. "I see," he said, and there followed a long silence.

The girl began buttoning and unbuttoning her glove. She must go; she was frightened, elated, amused. She did not want to go, but go she must. Would he ever forgive her?

"Don't--don't hate me!" she said.

Amory awoke from his stunned meditation. "My dear young lady, of course not," he began; "only, Tom will be terribly broken up. It's the only thing to do now, I suppose, but why did you do the other?"

She looked at him. As well be hanged for a sheep as a lamb, she thought. "I was unhappy and foolish." She hesitated. "But you needn't be troubled about Tom. He--" Again she hesitated.

"Not troubled about old Tom!" expostulated Amory.

"Wait." She put up her hand. "He made a mistake, too; he doesn't care so very much, and he has already flirted--"

Amory laid his hand on her chair. "Tom!"

"Yes," she repeated; "he really is rather a flirt, and--"

"Tom!"

She nodded. "Yes; really, it did hurt me a little, only--"

"Tom!"

She faced him. "Yes, Tom. What do you think Tom is--blind and deaf and dumb? Any man worth his salt can flirt."

Amory stared at her. "Oh, he can, can he?"

She nodded. "He was very good and kind, but I saw that he was changing; and then he met a little fair-haired, blue-eyed--"

Amory interposed. "I told you."

She gave him a curious smile. "Yes, a silly little blond thing, just that."

But his satisfaction in his perspicacity was short-lived; he walked up and down the room in his perplexity. "I can't get over it," he murmured. "I thought it a mad love-match, all done in a few weeks; and to have it turn out like this! You--"

"Mercenary," she interjected, with a sad little smile.

He looked at her. "Yes; and Tom--"

"Fickle," she ended again.

"Yes, and Tom fickle. Why, it shakes the foundations!"

The girl felt a sudden wave of shame and weariness. She must go. She hadn't been fair, but it had been so sudden, so difficult. She looked at him, and getting up, wondered if she would ever see him again.

"I must go," she said. "I came--" She hesitated, and a sudden desire to have him know her as herself swept over her. It needed only another lie or two in the beginning, and then some truth would come through to sustain her. She went on: "I came because I wanted to know what you were like; Tom had talked so much of you, and I wanted some one to understand and perhaps explain; and now I must go and leave your warm, delightful room for the comfortless place I live in. Don't think too hardly of me."

Amory shook his head. "You don't leave me until you have had your tea." He rang the bell. "But what do you mean by a comfortless home? Does Mrs. White neglect you?"

She looked at the fire. "I don't live with her--now; I live alone; I work for my living."

Amory got up as the maid brought in the tea-tray, and setting it beside them, he poured out her tea; as he handed her the cup, he brought his brows together sternly, as though making out her very mysterious words.

"You work for your living?" he repeated. "I thought you lived with Mrs. White, and that they were well off."

"I did, but now I've come back to my real life, which I would have left had I married Tom."

He nodded. "I see. I had heard awfully little about it all; I was away, and then it was so quickly done."

"I know," she went on, hurriedly; "but let me tell you, and you will understand me better later--that is, if you want to understand me."

"Most certainly I do." Amory sustained the strange sad gaze of her charming, heavy-lidded eyes in a sort of maze. Her mat skin looked white, now that her blushes were gone, and her delicate, irregular features a little pinched. He drank his tea and watched her while she talked.

"I teach music," she began; "to do it I left my relations in the country and came to this horrible great city. I have one dreary, cold room, as unlike this as two rooms can be. I have tried to make it seem like a home, but when I saw this I knew how I had failed."

"Poor little girl!" said Amory.

"I have the ordinary feelings of a girl," she went on, "and yet I see before me the long stretch of a dreary life. I love music; I hear none but the strumming of children. I like pictures, books, people; I see none. I like to laugh, to talk; there is no one to laugh with, to talk to. I am very--unhappy." The last words were spoken very low, but the misery in them touched Amory deeply.

"Poor little girl!" he said again, and gently laid his hand on the arm of her chair. "But how can Tom know this and let you go? You are mistaken in Tom, I am sure, and--"

The girl straightened her slender figure and rose. "Oh no! it is all right. He doesn't love me, your Tom; and so the world goes--I must go, too. I--"

"Don't go," said Amory. "Let me--" She shook her head. "You have no more to do; you have comforted and warmed and fed a hungry wanderer, and she must make haste home. Thank you for everything; thank you."

Amory felt a pang as she stood up. Not to see her again--why, that was absurd! Why should he not see her? She had quarrelled with Tom, yes, and perhaps the family might be hard on her; but he--he understood, and why should he shake off her acquaintance? She was not for Tom. Well, it was just as well. How could any one think this girl would suit Tom--big-bearded, clumsy, excellent fellow that he was?

He put out his hand. "Mary," he said. The girl stared at him with eyes suddenly wide open; he smiled into them.

"I have a right to call you that," he proceeded, "haven't I? I might have been your brother." He took her hand, and then laughed a little. "I am almost glad I am not. You wouldn't have suited Tom, and as a sister, somehow, you wouldn't have suited me!" He laughed again. "But"--he hesitated; she still stared straight up at him with her soft, dark eyes, and he thought them very beautiful--"but why shouldn't I see you--not as a brother, but an acquaintance--friend? You say you need them. Tell me where you have this room of yours?"

The vivid beauty of her blush startled him, and she drew her hand quickly from his.

"Oh no!" she said, hurriedly. "Let things drop between us; here--forever."

Amory stood before her with an expression which reminded her of his description of himself--obstinate; yes, he looked it.

"Why?" he urged. "Just because you are not to marry Tom, is there any reason why we should not like each other--is there? That is--if we do! I do," he laughed. "Do you?"

Her lids had dropped; she looked very slim, and young, and shy. "Yes," she said.

It gave Amory a good deal of pleasure for a monosyllable.

"Well, then, your number?" he said.

She shook her head.

"I'll ask Tom," he retorted. "He will tell me."

He was baffled and curiously charmed by the smile that touched her sharply curved young mouth.

"Tom may," she said.

"I was ready to accept you as a sister," he persisted, "and you won't even admit me as a casual visitor!"

She took a step toward the door. "Wait till you hear Tom's story," she said.

Amory stared curiously at her. "Do you think he will be vindictive, after all?" he said. "Why should he be, if what you say is just?"

She paused. "Wait till you see Tom and Mrs. White; then if you want to know me, why--" She was blushing again.

"Well," Amory demanded, "what shall I do?"

She looked up with a sort of childish charm, curling her lip, lighting her eyes with something of laughter and mischief. "Why, look for me and you'll find me."

"Find you?" repeated Amory, bewildered.

She nodded. "Yes, if you look. To-morrow will be Sunday; every one will be going to church, and I with them. Stand on the steps of this house at 10.30 precisely, and look as far as you can, and you will see--me. Goodnight."

"Good night." Amory took her hand. "Let me see you home; it's dark."

She laughed. "You don't lack persistency, do you?" she said, with a sweetness which gave the words a pleasant twist. "But don't come, please. I'm used to taking care of myself; but--before I go let me write my note also." She went to the desk and scratched a line, and folding it, handed it to him. "There," she said; "read Mrs. White's note and then that, but wait till you hear the house door bang. Promise not before."

"Please--" began Amory.

"Promise," she repeated.

"I promise," he said, and again they shook hands for good-by.

"That's three times," thought the girl as she went to the door, and turning an instant, she smiled at him. "Good-by." The door closed softly behind her, and Amory waited a moment, then went to it, and opening it, listened; the house door shut lightly, and seizing his notes, he stood by the window in the twilight and read them. The first was as follows:

"DEAR MR. AMORY,--Mary and I had to return unexpectedly to Cleveland. Forgive our missing this chance of meeting you, but Mr. White's note is urgent, as his sister is very ill. Mary regrets greatly not seeing you before the wedding.

Yours sincerely,

BARBARA WHITE."

Amory threw the paper down. "Do I see visions?" he cried, and hastily unfolded the second; it ran as follows:

"Forgive me; I got into the wrong house, the wrong room. I was very tired, and my latch-key fitted, and I didn't know until I saw your fire, and then you came. Don't think me a very bold and horrid girl, and forgive me. Your fire was so warm and bright, and--you were kind.

M."

Amory stared at the paper a moment; then, catching his hat and flying down the stairs, opened the outer door.

The night was bitter cold, with a white frost everywhere; but in the twilight no solitary figure was in view; the long street was empty. He ran the length of it, then back to his room, and throwing down his hat, he lit his pipe. It needed thought.

BRAYBRIDGE'S OFFER
WILLIAM DEAN HOWELLS

We had ordered our dinners and were sitting in the Turkish room at the club, waiting to be called, each in his turn, to the dining-room. With its mixture of Oriental appointments in curtains, cushions, and little tables of teak-wood the Turkish room expressed rather an adventurous conception of the Ottoman taste; but it was always a cozy place whether you found yourself in it with cigars and coffee after dinner, or with whatever liquid or solid appetizer you preferred in the half-hour or more that must pass before dinner after you had made out your menu. It intimated an exclusive possession in the three or four who happened first to find themselves together in it, and it invited the philosophic mind to contemplation more than any other spot in the club.

Our rather limited little down-town dining club was almost a celibate community at most times. A few husbands and fathers joined us at lunch; but at dinner we were nearly always a company of bachelors, dropping in an hour or so before we wished to dine, and ordering from a bill of fare what we liked. Some dozed away the intervening time; some read the evening papers, or played chess; I preferred the chance society of the Turkish room. I could be pretty sure of finding Wanhope there in these sympathetic moments, and where Wanhope was there would probably be Rulledge, passively willing to listen and agree, and Minver ready to interrupt and dispute. I myself liked to look in and linger for either the reasoning or the bickering, as it happened, and now seeing the three there together, I took a provisional seat behind the painter, who made no sign of knowing I was present. Rulledge was eating a caviar sandwich, which he had brought from the afternoon tea-table near by, and he greedily incited Wanhope to go on, in the polite pause which the psychologist had let follow on my appearance, with what he was saying. I was not surprised to find that his talk related to a fact just then intensely interesting to the few, rapidly becoming the many, who were privy to it; though Wanhope had the air of stooping to it from a higher range of thinking.

"I shouldn't have supposed, somehow," he said with a knot of deprecation between his fine eyes, "that he would have had the pluck."

"Perhaps he hadn't," Minver suggested.

Wanhope waited for a thoughtful moment of censure eventuating in toleration. "You mean that she--"

"I don't see why you say that, Minver," Rulledge interposed chivalrously, with his mouth full of sandwich.

"I didn't say it," Minver contradicted.

"You implied it; and I don't think it's fair. It's easy enough to build up a report of that kind on the half-knowledge of rumor which is all that any outsider can have in the case."

"So far," Minver said, with unbroken tranquillity, "as any such edifice has been erected, you are the architect, Rulledge. I shouldn't think you would like to go round insinuating that sort of thing. Here is Acton," and he now acknowledged my presence with a backward twist of his head, "on the alert for material already. You ought to be more careful where Acton is, Rulledge."

"It would be great copy if it were true," I owned.

Wanhope regarded us all three, in this play of our qualities, with the scientific impartiality of a bacteriologist in the study of a culture offering some peculiar incidents. He took up a point as remote as might be from the personal appeal. "It is curious how little we know of such matters, after all the love-making and marrying in life and all the inquiry of the poets and novelists." He addressed himself in this turn of his thought, half playful, half earnest, to me, as if I united with the functions of both a responsibility for their shortcomings.

"Yes," Minver said, facing about toward me. "How do you excuse yourself for your ignorance in matters where you're always professionally making such a bluff of knowledge? After all the marriages you have brought about in literature, can you say positively and specifically how they are brought about in life?"

"No, I can't," I admitted. "I might say that a writer of fiction is a good deal like a minister who continually marries people without knowing why."

"No, you couldn't, my dear fellow," the painter retorted. "It's part of your swindler to assume that you *do* know why. You ought to find out."

Wanhope interposed abstractly, or as abstractly as he could: "The important thing would always be to find which of the lovers the confession, tacit or explicit, began with."

"Acton ought to go round and collect human documents bearing on the question. He ought to have got together thousands of specimens from nature. He ought to have gone to all the married couples he knew, and asked them just how their passion was confessed; he ought to have sent out printed circulars, with tabulated questions. Why don't you do it, Acton?"

I returned, as seriously as could have been expected: "Perhaps it would be thought rather intimate. People don't like to talk of such things."

"They're ashamed," Minver declared. "The lovers don't either of them, in a given ease, like to let others know how much the woman had to do with making the offer, and how little the man."

Minver's point provoked both Wanhope and myself to begin a remark at the same time. We begged each other's pardon, and Wanhope insisted that I should go on.

"Oh, merely this," I said. "I don't think they're so much ashamed as that they have forgotten the different stages. You were going to say?"

"Very much what you said. It's astonishing how people forget the vital things, and remember trifles. Or perhaps as we advance from stage to stage what once seemed the vital things turn to trifles. Nothing can be more vital in the history of a man and a woman than how they became husband and wife, and yet not merely the details, but the main fact, would seem to escape record if not recollection. The next generation knows nothing of it."

"That appears to let Acton out," Minver said. "But how do *you* know what you were saying, Wanhope?"

"I've ventured to make some inquiries in that region at one time. Not directly, of course. At second and third hand. It isn't inconceivable, if we conceive of a life after this, that a man should forget, in its more important interests and occupations, just how he quitted this world, or at least the particulars of the article of death. Of course, we must suppose a good portion of eternity to have elapsed." Wanhope continued, dreamily, with a deep breath almost equivalent to something so unscientific as a sigh: "Women are charming, and in nothing more than the perpetual challenge they form for us. They are born defying us to match ourselves with them."

"Do you mean that Miss Hazelwood--" Rulledge began, but Minver's laugh arrested him.

"Nothing so concrete, I'm afraid," Wanhope gently returned. "I mean, to match them in graciousness, in loveliness, in all the agile contests of spirit and plays of fancy. There's something pathetic to see them caught up into something more serious in that other game, which they are so good at."

"They seem rather to like it, though, some of them, if you mean the game of love," Minver said. "Especially when they're not in earnest about it."

"Oh, there are plenty of spoiled women," Wanhope admitted. "But I don't mean flirting. I suppose that the average unspoiled woman is rather frightened than otherwise when she knows that a man is in love with her."

"Do you suppose she always knows it first?" Rulledge asked.

"You may be sure," Minver answered for Wanhope, "that if she didn't know it, *he* never would." Then Wanhope answered for himself:

"I think that generally she sees it coming. In that sort of wireless telegraphy, that reaching out of two natures through space towards each other, her more sensitive apparatus probably feels the appeal of his before he is conscious of having made any appeal."

"And her first impulse is to escape the appeal?" I suggested.

"Yes," Wanhope admitted after a thoughtful reluctance.

"Even when she is half aware of having invited it?"

"If she is not spoiled she is never aware of having invited it. Take the case in point; we won't mention any names. She is sailing through time, through youthful space, with her electrical lures, the natural equipment of every charming woman, all out, and suddenly, somewhere from the unknown, she feels the shock of a response in the gulfs of air where there had been no life before. But she can't be said to have knowingly searched the void for any presence."

"Oh, I'm not sure about that, professor," Minver put in. "Go a little slower, if you expect me to follow you."

"It's all a mystery, the most beautiful mystery of life," Wanhope resumed. "I don't believe I could make out the case, as I feel it to be."

"Braybridge's part of the case is rather plain, isn't it?" I invited him.

"I'm not sure of that. No man's part of any case is plain, if you look at it carefully. The most that you can say of Braybridge is that he is rather a simple nature. But nothing," the psychologist added with one of his deep breaths, "is so complex as a simple nature."

"Well," Minver contended, "Braybridge is plain, if his case isn't."

"Plain? Is he plain?" Wanhope asked, as if asking himself.

"My dear fellow, you agnostics doubt everything!"

"I should have said picturesque. Picturesque, with the sort of unbeautifulness that takes the fancy of women more than Greek proportion. I think it would require a girl peculiarly feminine to feel the attraction of such a man--the fascination of his being grizzled, and slovenly, and rugged. She would have to be rather a wild, shy girl to do that, and it would have to be through her fear of him that she would divine his fear of her. But what I have heard is that they met under rather exceptional circumstances. It was at a house in the Adirondacks, where Braybridge was, somewhat in the quality of a bull in a china-shop. He was lugged in by the host, as an old friend, and was suffered by the hostess as a friend quite too old for her. At any rate, as I heard (and I don't vouch for the facts, all of them), Braybridge found himself at odds with the gay young people who made up the hostess's end of the party, and was watching for a chance to--"

Wanhope cast about for the word, and Winver supplied it: "Pull out."

"Yes. But when he had found it Miss Hazelwood took it from him."

"I don't understand," Rulledge said.

"When he came in to breakfast, the third morning, prepared with an excuse for cutting his week down to the dimensions it had reached, he saw her sitting alone at the table. She had risen early as a consequence of having arrived late, the night before; and when Braybridge found himself in for it, be forgot that he meant to go away, and said good-morning, as if they knew each other. Their hostess found them talking over the length of the table in a sort of mutual fright, and introduced them. But it's rather difficult reporting a lady verbatim at second hand. I really had the facts from Welkin, who had them from his wife. The sum of her impressions was that Braybridge and Miss Hazelwood were getting a kind of comfort out of their mutual terror because one was as badly frightened as the other. It was a novel experience for both. Ever seen her?"

We others looked at each other. Minver said: "I never wanted to paint any one so much. It was at the spring show of the American Artists. There was a jam of people; but this girl--I've understood it was she--looked as much alone as if there were nobody else there. She might have been a startled doe in the North Woods suddenly coming out on a twenty-thousand-dollar camp, with a lot of twenty-million-dollar people on the veranda."

"And you wanted to do her as The Startled Doe," I said. "Good selling name."

"Don't reduce it to the vulgarity of fiction. I admit it would be a selling name."

"Go on, Wanhope," Rulledge puffed impatiently. "Though I don't see how there could be another soul in the universe as constitutionally scared of men as Braybridge is of women."

"In the universe nothing is wasted, I suppose. Everything has its complement, its response. For every bashful man, there must be a bashful woman," Wanhope returned.

"Or a bold one," Minver suggested.

"No; the response must be in kind, to be truly complemental. Through the sense of their reciprocal timidity they divine that they needn't be afraid."

"Oh! *That's* the way you get out of it!"

"Well?" Rulledge urged.

"I'm afraid," Wanhope modestly confessed, "that from this point I shall have to be largely conjectural. Welkin wasn't able to be very definite, except as to moments, and he had his data almost altogether from his wife. Braybridge had told him overnight that he thought of going, and he had said he mustn't think of it; but he supposed Braybridge had spoken of it to Mrs. Welkin, and he began by saying to his wife that he hoped she had refused to hear of Braybridge's going. She said she hadn't heard of it, but now she would refuse without hearing, and she didn't give Braybridge any chance to protest. If people went in the middle of their week, what would become of other people? She was not going to have the equilibrium of her party disturbed, and that was all about it. Welkin thought it was odd that

Braybridge didn't insist; and he made a long story of it. But the grain of wheat in his bushel of chaff was that Miss Hazelwood seemed to be fascinated by Braybridge from the first. When Mrs. Welkin scared him into saying that he would stay his week out, the business practically was done. They went picnicking that day in each other's charge; and after Braybridge left he wrote back to her, as Mrs. Welkin knew from the letters that passed through her hands, and--Well, their engagement has come out, and--" Wanhope paused with an air that was at first indefinite, and then definitive.

"You don't mean," Rulledge burst out in a note of deep wrong, "that that's all you know about it?"

"Yes, that's all I know," Wanhope confessed, as if somewhat surprised himself at the fact.

"Well!"

Wanhope tried to offer the only reparation in his power. "I can conjecture--we can all conjecture--"

He hesitated; then, "Well, go on with your conjecture," Rulledge said forgivingly.

"Why--" Wanhope began again; but at that moment a man who had been elected the year before, and then gone off on a long absence, put his head in between the dull-red hangings of the doorway. It was Halson, whom I did not know very well, but liked better than I knew. His eyes were dancing with what seemed the inextinguishable gayety of his temperament, rather than any present occasion, and his smile carried his little mustache well away from his handsome teeth. "Private?"

"Come in, come in!" Minver called to him. "Thought you were in Japan?"

"My dear fellow," Halson answered, "you must brush up your contemporary history. It's more than a fortnight since I was in Japan." He shook hands with me, and I introduced him to Rulledge and Wanhope. He said at once: "Well, what is it? Question of Braybridge's engagement? It's humiliating to a man to come back from the antipodes, and find the nation absorbed in a parochial problem like that. Everybody I've met here to-night has asked me, the first thing, if I'd heard of it, and if I knew how it could have happened."

"And do you?" Rulledge asked.

"I can give a pretty good guess," Halson said, running his merry eyes over our faces.

"Anybody can give a good guess," Rulledge said. "Wanhope is doing it now."

"Don't let me interrupt." Halson turned to him politely.

"Not at all. I'd rather hear your guess. If you know Braybridge better than I," Wanhope said.

"Well," Halson compromised, "perhaps I've known him longer." He asked, with an effect of coming to business, "Where were you?"

"Tell him, Rulledge," Minver ordered, and Rulledge apparently asked nothing better. He told him in detail, all we knew from any source, down to the moment of Wanhope's arrested conjecture.

"He did leave you at an anxious point, didn't he?" Halson smiled to the rest of us at Rulledge's expense, and then said: "Well, I think I can help you out a little. Any of you know the lady?"

"By sight, Minver does," Rulledge answered for us. "Wants to paint her." "Of course," Halson said, with intelligence. "But I doubt if he'd find her as paintable as she looks, at first. She's beautiful, but her charm is spiritual."

"Sometimes we try for that," the painter interposed.

"And sometimes you get it. But you'll allow it's difficult. That's all I meant. I've known her--let me see--for twelve years, at least; ever since I first went West. She was about eleven then, and her father was bringing her up on the ranche. Her aunt came along, by and by, and took her to Europe; mother dead before Hazelwood went out there. But the girl was always homesick for the ranche; she pined for it; and after they had kept her in Germany three or four years they let her come back, and run wild again; wild as a flower does, or a vine--not a domesticated animal."

"Go slow, Halson. This is getting too much for the romantic Rulledge."

"Rulledge can bear up against the facts, I guess, Minver," Halson said, almost austerely. "Her father died two years ago, and then she **had** to come East, for her aunt simply **wouldn't** live on the ranche. She brought her on, here, and brought her out; I was at the coming-out tea; but the girl didn't take to the New York thing at all; I could see it from the start; she wanted to get away from it with me, and talk about the ranche."

"She felt that she was with the only genuine person among those conventional people."

Halson laughed at Minver's thrust, and went on amiably: "I don't suppose that till she met Braybridge she was ever quite at her ease with any man or woman, for that matter. I imagine, as you've done, that it was his fear of her that gave her courage. She met him on equal terms. Isn't that it?"

Wanhope assented to the question referred to him with a nod.

"And when they got lost from the rest of the party at that picnic--"

"Lost?" Rulledge demanded.

"Why, yes. Didn't you know? But I ought to go back. They said there never was anything prettier than the way she unconsciously went for Braybridge, the whole day. She wanted him, and she was a child who wanted things frankly, when she did want them. Then his being ten or fifteen years older than she was, and so large and simple, made it natural for a shy girl like her to assort herself with him when all the rest were assorting themselves, as people do at such things. The consensus of testimony is that she did it with the most transparent unconsciousness, and--"

"Who are your authorities?" Minver asked; Rulledge threw himself back on the divan, and beat the cushions with impatience.

"Is it essential to give them?"

"Oh, no. I merely wondered. Go on."

"The authorities are all right. She had disappeared with him before the others noticed. It was a thing that happened; there was no design in it; that would have been out of character. They had got to the end of the wood-road, and into the thick of the trees where there wasn't even a trail, and they walked round looking for a way out, till they were turned completely. They decided that the only way was to keep walking, and by and by they heard the sound of chopping. It was some Canucks clearing a piece of the woods, and when she spoke to them in French, they gave them full directions, and Braybridge soon found the path again."

Halson paused, and I said, "But that isn't all?"

"Oh, no." He continued thoughtfully silent for a little while before he resumed. "The amazing thing is that they got lost again, and that when they tried going back to the Canucks, they couldn't find the way."

"Why didn't they follow the sound of the chopping?" I asked.

"The Canucks had stopped, for the time being. Besides, Braybridge was rather ashamed, and he thought if they went straight on they would be sure to come out somewhere. But that was where he made a mistake. They couldn't go on straight; they went round and round, and came on their own footsteps--or hers, which he recognized from the narrow tread and the dint of the little heels in the damp places."

Wanhope roused himself with a kindling eye. "That is very interesting, the movement in a circle of people who have lost their way. It has often been observed, but I don't know that it has ever been explained. Sometimes the circle is smaller, sometimes it is larger; but I believe it is always a circle."

"Isn't it," I queried, "like any other error in life? We go round and round; and commit the old sins over again."

"That is very interesting," Wanhope allowed.

"But do lost people really always walk in a vicious circle?" Minver asked.

Rulledge would not let Wanhope answer. "Go on, Halson," he said.

Halson roused himself from the reverie in which he was sitting with glazed eyes. "Well, what made it a little more anxious was that he had heard of bears on that mountain, and the green afternoon light among the trees was perceptibly paling. He suggested shouting, but she wouldn't let him; she said it would be ridiculous, if the others heard them, and useless if they didn't. So they tramped on till--till the accident happened."

"The accident!" Rulledge exclaimed in the voice of our joint emotion.

"He stepped on a loose stone and turned his foot," Halson explained. "It wasn't a sprain, luckily, but it hurt enough. He turned so white that she noticed it, and asked him what was the matter. Of course that shut his mouth the closer, but it morally doubled his motive, and he kept himself from crying out till the sudden pain of the wrench was over. He said merely that he thought he had heard something, and he had--an awful ringing in his ears; but he didn't mean that, and he started on again. The worst was trying to walk without limping, and to talk cheerfully and encouragingly, with that agony tearing at him. But he managed somehow, and he was congratulating himself on his success, when he tumbled down in a dead faint."

"Oh, come, now!" Minver protested.

"It *is* like an old-fashioned story, where things are operated by accident instead of motive, isn't it?" Halson smiled with radiant recognition.

"Fact will always imitate fiction, if you give her time enough," I said.

"Had they got back to the other picnickers?" Rulledge asked with a tense voice.

"In sound, but not in sight of them. She wasn't going to bring him into camp in that state; besides she couldn't. She got some water out of the trout-brook they'd been fishing--more water than trout in it--and sprinkled his face, and he came to, and got on his legs, just in time to pull on to the others, who were organizing a search-party to go after them. From that point on, she dropped Braybridge like a hot coal, and as there was nothing of the flirt in her, she simply kept with the women, the older girls, and the tabbies, and left Braybridge to worry along with the secret of his turned ankle. He doesn't know how he ever got home alive; but he did somehow manage to reach the wagons that had brought them to the edge of the woods, and then he was all right till they got to the house. But still she said nothing about his accident, and be couldn't; and he pleaded an early start for town the next morning, and got off to bed, as soon as he could."

"I shouldn't have thought he could have stirred in the morning," Rulledge employed Halson's pause to say.

"Well, this beaver **had** to," Halson said. "He was not the only early riser. He found Miss Hazelwood at the station before him."

"What!" Rulledge shouted. I confess the fact rather roused me, too; and Wanhope's eyes kindled with a scientific pleasure.

"She came right towards him. 'Mr. Braybridge,' says she, 'I couldn't let you go without explaining my very strange behavior. I didn't choose to have these people laughing at the notion of **my** having played the part of your preserver. It was bad enough being lost with you; I couldn't bring you into ridicule with them by the disproportion they'd have felt in my efforts for you after you turned your foot. So I simply had to ignore the incident. Don't you see?' Braybridge glanced at her, and he had never felt so big and bulky before, or seen her so slender and little. He said, 'It **would** have seemed rather absurd,' and he broke out and laughed, while she broke down and cried, and asked him to forgive her, and whether it had hurt him very much; and said she knew he could bear to keep it from the others by the way he had kept it from her till he fainted. She implied that he was morally as well as physically gigantic, and it was as much as he could do to keep from taking her in his arms on the spot."

"It would have been edifying to the groom that had driven her to the station," Minver cynically suggested.

"Groom nothing!" Halson returned with spirit. "She paddled herself across the lake, and walked from the boat-landing to the station."

"Jove!" Rulledge exploded in uncontrollable enthusiasm.

"She turned round as soon as she had got through with her hymn of praise--it made Braybridge feel awfully flat--and ran back through the bushes to the boat-landing, and--that was the last he saw of her till he met her in town this fall."

"And when--and when--did he offer himself?" Rulledge entreated breathlessly. "How--"

"Yes, that's the point, Halson," Minver interposed. "Your story is all very well, as far as it goes; but Rulledge here has been insinuating that it was Miss Hazelwood who made the offer, and he wants you to bear him out."

Rulledge winced at the outrage, but he would not stay Halson's answer even for the sake of righting himself.

"I *have* heard," Minver went on, "that Braybridge insisted on paddling the canoe back to the other shore for her, and that it was on the way that he offered himself." We others stared at Minver in astonishment. Halson glanced covertly toward him with his gay eyes. "Then that wasn't true?"

"How did you hear it?" Halson asked.

"Oh, never mind. Is it true?"

"Well, I know there's that version," Halson said evasively. "The engagement is only just out, as you know. As to the offer--the when and the how--I don't know that I'm exactly at liberty to say."

"I don't see why," Minver urged. "You might stretch a point for Rulledge's sake."

Halson looked down, and then he glanced at Minver after a furtive passage of his eye over Rulledge's intense face. "There was something rather nice happened after--But really, now!"

"Oh, go on!" Minver called out in contempt of his scruple.

"I haven't the right--Well, I suppose I'm on safe ground here? It won't go any farther, of course; and it *was* so pretty! After she had pushed off in her canoe, you know, Braybridge--he'd followed her down to the shore of the lake--found her

handkerchief in a bush where it had caught, and he held it up, and called out to
her. She looked round and saw it, and called back: 'Never mind. I can't return for
it, now.' Then Braybridge plucked up his courage, and asked if he might keep it,
and she said 'Yes,' over her shoulder, and then she stopped paddling, and said 'No,
no, you mustn't, you mustn't! You can send it to me.' He asked where, and she
said, 'In New York--in the fall--at the Walholland.' Braybridge never knew how he
dared, but he shouted after her--she was paddling on again--'May I **bring** it?' and
she called over her shoulder again, without fully facing him, but her profile was
enough, 'If you can't get any one to bring it for you.' The words barely reached him,
but he'd have caught them if they'd been whispered; and he watched her across the
lake, and into the bushes, and then broke for his train. He was just in time."

Halson beamed for pleasure upon us, and even Minver said, "Yes, that's rather
nice." After a moment he added, "Rulledge thinks she put it there."

"You're too bad, Minver," Halson protested. "The charm of the whole thing
was her perfect innocence. She isn't capable of the slightest finesse. I've known her
from a child, and I know what I say."

"That innocence of girlhood," Wanhope said, "is very interesting. It's astonishing how much experience it survives. Some women carry it into old age with them.
It's never been scientifically studied--"

"Yes," Minver allowed. "There would be a fortune for the novelist who could
work a type of innocence for all it was worth. Here's Acton always dealing with
the most rancid flirtatiousness, and missing the sweetness and beauty of a girlhood
which does the cheekiest things without knowing what it's about, and fetches down
its game whenever it shuts its eyes and fires at nothing. But I don't see how all this
touches the point that Rulledge makes, or decides which finally made the offer."

"Well, hadn't the offer already been made?"

"But how?"

"Oh, in the usual way."

"What is the usual way?"

"I thought everybody knew **that**. Of course, it was **from** Braybridge finally,
but I suppose it's always six of one and half a dozen of the other in these cases, isn't
it? I dare say he couldn't get any one to take her the handkerchief. My dinner?"
Halson looked up at the silent waiter who had stolen upon us and was bowing to-

ward him.

"Look here, Halson," Minver detained him, "how is it none of the rest of us have heard all those details?"

"I don't know where you've been, Minver. Everybody knows the main facts," Halson said, escaping.

Wanhope observed musingly: "I suppose he's quite right about the reciprocality of the offer, as we call it. There's probably, in ninety-nine cases out of a hundred, a perfect understanding before there's an explanation. In many cases the offer and the acceptance must really be tacit."

"Yes," I ventured, "and I don't know why we're so severe with women when they seem to take the initiative. It's merely, after all, the call of the maiden bird, and there's nothing lovelier or more endearing in nature than that."

"Maiden bird is good, Acton," Minver approved. "Why don't you institute a class of fiction, where the love-making is all done by the maiden birds, as you call them--or the widow birds? It would be tremendously popular with both sexes. It would lift a tremendous responsibility off the birds who've been expected to shoulder it heretofore if it could be introduced into real life."

Rulledge fetched a long, simple-hearted sigh. "Well, it's a charming story. How well he told it!"

The waiter came again, and this time signalled to Minver.

"Yes," he said, as he rose. "What a pity you can't believe a word Halson says."

"Do you mean--" we began simultaneously.

"That be built the whole thing from the ground up, with the start that we had given him. Why, you poor things! Who could have told him how it all happened? Braybridge? Or the girl? As Wanhope began by saying, people don't speak of their love-making, even when they distinctly remember it."

"Yes, but see here, Minver!" Rulledge said with a dazed look. "If it's all a fake of his, how came *you* to have heard of Braybridge paddling the canoe back for her?"

"That was the fake that tested the fake. When he adopted it, I *knew* he was lying, because I was lying myself. And then the cheapness of the whole thing! I wonder that didn't strike you. It's the stuff that a thousand summer-girl stories have been spun out of. Acton might have thought he was writing it!"

He went away, leaving us to a blank silence, till Wanhope managed to say:

"That inventive habit of mind is very curious. It would be interesting to know just how far it imposes on the inventor himself--how much he believes of his own fiction."

"I don't see," Rulledge said gloomily, "why they're so long with my dinner." Then he burst out, "I believe every word Halson said. If there's any fake in the thing, it's the fake that Minver owned to."

THE RUBAIYAT AND THE LINER
ELIA W. PEATTIE

C hug-chug, chug-chug!"
That was the liner, and it had been saying the same thing for two nights and two days. Therefore nobody paid any attention to it--except Chalmers Payne, the moodiest of the passengers, who noticed it and said to himself that, for his part, it did as well as any other sound, and was much better than most persons' conversation.

It will be guessed that Mr. Chalmers Payne was in an irritable frame of mind. He was even retaliative, and to the liner's continued iteration of its innocent remark he retorted in the words of old Omar:

"Perplext no more with Human or Divine,
To-morrow's tangle to the winds resign,
And lose your fingers in the tresses of
The cypress-slender Minister of Wine.
  "And if the wine you drink, the Lip you press,
End in what All begins and ends in--Yes;
Think then you are To-day what Yesterday
You were--To-morrow you shall not be less.
  "So when the Angel of the Darker Drink
At last shall find you by the River-brink,
And, offering his Cup, invite your Soul
Forth to your Lips to quaff--you shall not shrink."

To these melancholy mutterings, the liner, insouciant, and not caring a peg for any philosophy--save that of the open road--shouldered along through jewel-green waves, and remarked, "Chug-chug, chug-chug!"

Mr. Payne was inclined to quarrel with the Tent-Maker on one score only. He did not think that he was to-day what he was yesterday. Yesterday--figuratively speaking--he had hope. He was conscious of his youth. A fine, buoyant egotism sustained him, and he believed that he was about to be crowned with a beautiful joy.

He had sauntered up to his joy, so to speak, cocksure, hands in pockets, and as he smiled with easy assurance, behold the joy turned into a sorrow. The face of the dryad smiling through the young grape leaves was that of a withered hag, and the leaves of the vine were dead and flapped on sapless stems!

Well, well, there was always a sorry fatalism to comfort one in joy's despite.

> "Then to the rolling Heav'n itself, I cried,
> Asking, 'What Lamp had Destiny to guide
> Her little Children stumbling in the Dark?'"

The answer was old as patience--as old as courage. But to theorize about it was really superfluous! Why think at all? Why not say chug-chug like the liner?

> "We are no other than a moving row
> Of Magic Shadow-shapes that come and go--"

Dinner! Was it possible? The day had been a blur! Well, probably all the rest of life would be a blur. Anyway, one could still dine, and he recollected that the puree of tomatoes at last night's dinner had been rather to his liking. He seated himself deliberately at the board, congratulating himself that he would be allowed to go through the duty of eating without interruption. The place at his right had been vacant ever since they left Southampton. At his left was a gentleman of uncertain hearing and a bullet-proof frown.

As the seat at his right had been vacant so long, he took the liberty of laying it his gloves, his sea-glass, a book with uncut leaves, and a crimson silk neck-scarf.

"I beg your pardon," said the waiter, "but the lady who is to sit here is coming, sir."

"The devil she is!" thought Payne. "Will the creature expect me to talk? Will she require me to look after her in the matter of pepper and salt? Why couldn't I have been left in peace?"

He gathered up his possessions, and arose gravely with an automatic courtesy, and lifted eyes with a wooden expression to stare at the intruder.

He faced the one person in the world whom it was most of pain and happiness to meet--the woman between whom and himself he meant to put a good half of the round world; and he read in her troubled gray eyes the confession that if there was anything or anybody from which she would willingly have been protected it was he--Chalmers Payne.

Conscious of their neighbors, they bowed. Payne saw her comfortably seated. He sat down and slowly emptied his glass of ice-water. He preserved his wooden expression of countenance and turned towards her.

"The old man on my right is deaf," he said.

"So am I," she retorted.

"Not so deaf, I hope, that you won't hear me explain that I had no more notion of your being on this ship than of Sappho being here!"

"You refer to--the Greek Sappho, Mr. Payne?"

"Assuredly. You told me--'fore Heaven, why are women so inconsistent?--you told me you were going anywhere rather than to America--that you were at the beginning of your journeyings--that you had an engagement with some Mahatmas on the top of the Himal--"

"And you--you were going to South Africa."

"I said nothing of the sort. I--"

"Well, I couldn't go about another day. No matter whether I was consistent or inconsistent! I was worn out and ill. I've been seeing too much--"

"You told me you could never see enough!"

"Well, never mind all that. I acted impulsively, I confess. My aunt was shocked. She thought I was ungrateful--particularly when I openly rejoiced that she was not able to find a chaperon for me."

"It's none of my business, anyway. I was stupid to show my surprise. I ought never to be surprised at anything you do, I know that. As for me, I'm tired of imitating the Wandering Jew. Besides, my father's old partner--mine he is now, I suppose, though I can't get used to that idea--wants me to come home. He says I'm needed. So I'm rolling up my sleeves, figuratively speaking. But I should certainly have delayed my journey if I had guessed you were to be on this boat."

"It's very annoying altogether," she said, with open vexation. "It looks so silly! What will my aunt say?"

"I don't think she'll say anything. You are on an Atlantic liner, with nine hundred and ninety-nine souls who are nothing to you, and one who is less than nothing. I believe that was the expression you used the other day--less than nothing?"

The girl's delicate face flushed hotly.

"I'm not so strong," she murmured. "It's true that I am worn out, and my voyage has done nothing so far towards restoring me. On the contrary, I have been suffering. I fainted again and again yesterday, and it took a great deal of courage for me to venture out to-day. So you must be merciful for a little while. Your enemy is down, you see."

"My enemy!" He gave the words an accent at once bitter and humorous. "I'll not say another personal word," he murmured, contritely. "Tell me if you feel faint at any moment, and let me help you. Please treat me as if I were your--your uncle!"

She smiled faintly.

"You are asking a great deal," she couldn't help saying, somewhat coquettishly, and then he remembered how he had seen her hanging about her uncle's neck, and he flushed too.

There was quite a long silence. She picked at her food delicately, and Payne suggested some claret. Her face showed that she would have preferred not to accept any favor from him, no matter how trifling, but she evidently considered it puerile to refuse.

"It *is* mighty awkward for you!" he burst out, suddenly, "my being here. I suppose you actually find it hard to believe that it was an accident--"

"I haven't the least occasion to doubt your word, Mr. Payne. Have I ever done anything to make you suppose that I didn't respect you?"

"Oh, I didn't mean that! Heavens! what a cad you must think me! I have a faculty for being stupid when you are around, you know. It's my misfortune. But-- behold my generosity!--I shall have a talk with the purser, Miss Curtis, and get him to change my place for me. Some good-natured person will consent to make the alteration"

"You mean you will put some one else here in your place beside me?"

"It's the least I can do, isn't it? Now, whom would you suggest? Pick out some-body. There's that motherly-looking German woman over there. She's a baron-ess--"

"She? She'll tell me twice every meal that American girls are not brought up with a knowledge of cooking. She will tell me how she has met them at Kaffee-klatsches, and how they confessed that they didn't cook! No, no; you must try an-other one!"

"Well, if you object to her, there's that quiet gentleman who is eating his ice with the aid of two pairs of spectacles. That gentleman is a specialist in bacilli. He has little steel-bound bottles in his room which, if you were to break them among this ship-load of passengers, would depopulate the ship. I think he is taking home the bacilli of the bubonic plague as a present to our country. Remember, if you got on the right side of him, that you would have a vengeance beyond the dreams of the Borgias at your command!"

"Oh, the terrible creature! Mr. Payne, how could you mention him? What if he were to take me for a guinea-pig or a rabbit? No, I prefer the English-looking mummy over there."

"Who? Miss Hull? She's not half bad. She's a great traveller. She has been al-most everywhere, and is now hastening to make it everywhere. She carries her own tea with her, and steeps it at five exactly every afternoon. She tells me that once, being shipwrecked, she grasped her tea-caddy, her alcohol-stove, and a large bottle of alcohol, and prepared for the worst. They drifted four days on a raft, and she made five-o'clock tea every day, to the great encouragement of the unfortunates. Miss Hull is an English spinster, who has a fortune and no household, and who is going about to see how other folks keep house--Feejee-Islanders, and Tagals, and Kafirs. She likes them all, I believe. Indeed, she says she likes everything--except the snug English village where she was brought up. She says that when she lived there she did exactly the same thing between sunup and sundown for eight years. For example, she had the curate to tea every Wednesday evening during that entire time, and when possible she had periwinkles."

"And nothing came of it?"

"Oh yes, an enormous consumption of tea-biscuits-nothing more. Then it oc-curred to her to travel. So she went to the next shire, and liked it so well that she plunged off to London, then to the Hebrides. After that there was no stopping her. She likes the islands better than the continents, and is collecting hats made of sea-grass. She already has five hundred and forty-two varieties. Really, you would not find her half so bad."

Helen Curtis finished her coffee, and laid her napkin beside her plate.

"Oh, if it comes to the negative virtues, you haven't been so disagreeable your-self to-day as you might have been. I'm under obligations to you. It **was** rather nice to meet an old acquaintance."

The tone was formal, and put Payne ten thousand leagues away from her. "Thank you," he said, with mock gratitude. "I'm under obligations for your cour-tesy, madam." She dropped her handkerchief as she arose, and he picked up the trifle and gave it to her. Their fingers met, and he withdrew his hand with a quick gesture.

"You must allow me to see you safely to your room," he urged. "Or else to your deck chair."

"Thank you. I'll go on deck, I think, and you may call the boy to go for my rug."

He put her on the lee side, and wrapped her in a McCallum plaid, and brought her some magazines from his own stateroom. Then he stood erect and saluted.

"Madam, have I the honor to be dismissed?"

She looked up and gave a friendly smile in spite of herself.

"You are very good," she said. "I am always remembering that you are good, and the thought annoys me."

"Oh, it needn't," he responded, in a philosophic tone, looking off towards the jagged line of the horizon, where the purple waves showed their changing outline. "If you are wondering why it is that you dislike me when you find nothing of which to disapprove in my conduct, don't let that puzzle you any longer. Regard does not depend upon character. The mystery of attraction has never been solved. Now, I've seen women more beautiful than you; I know many who are more learned; as for a sense of justice and fairness, why, I don't think you understand the first principles. Yet you are the one woman, in the world for me. Now that you've taken love out of my life, this world is nothing more to me than a workshop. I shall get up every morning and put myself at my bench, so to speak, and work till nightfall. Then I shall sleep. It is dull, but it doesn't matter. I have been at some trouble to convince myself of the fact that it doesn't matter, and I value the conviction. Life isn't as disheartening as it would be if it lasted longer.

> "'Tis but a Tent where takes his one day's rest
> A Sultan to the realms of Death addrest;
> The Sultan rises, and the dark Ferrash
> Strikes, and prepares it for another guest."

Miss Curtis sat up in her chair, and her eyes were flashing indignation.

"I won't listen in silence to the profanity of that old heathen," she cried.

"You refer to my friend Omar?" inquired Paine, quizzically, dropping his earnestness as soon as she assumed it.

"I consider him one of the most dangerous of men! Once you would have been above advancing such philosophy! The idea of your talking that inert fatalism! It's incredible that you should admire what is supine and cowardly--"

Payne's eyes were twinkling. He lit his pipe with a "By your permission," and between the puffs chanted:

> "Ah, Love! could thou and I with Fate conspire
> To grasp this sorry scheme of Things entire
> Would we not shatter it to bits--and then
> Remould it nearer to the Heart's Desire!"

"Even that is blasphemous impertinence!" the lady protested, knowing that she was angry, and rejoicing in the sensation.

"You think so?" cried Payne, not waiting for her to finish. "Why did you complain, then, of taking up the burden of common things? Do you want to be reminded of what you told me? You said that the roving life you had been leading in Europe for the past two years had unsettled you. You said you wanted to live among the old things and the dreams of old things. You liked the sense of irresponsible delight, and weren't prepared to say that you could ever assume the dull domestic round in a commonplace town. You considered the love of one human creature altogether too small and banal a thing to make you forego your intellectual incursions into the lands of delight. You were of the opinion that you loved many thousand creatures, most of them dead, and to enjoy their society to the full it was necessary for you to look at the cathedrals they had builded, to read the books they had written, or gaze upon the canvases they had painted. You were in a poppy sleep on the mystic flowers of ancient dreams. Wasn't that it? So I, a mere practical, every-day fellow, who had shown an unaccountable weakness in staying away from home a full year longer than I had any business to, was to go back alone to my work and my empty house, and console myself with the day's work. You were to go walking along the twilight path where the half-gods had walked before you, and I was to trudge up a dusty road fringed with pusley, and ending in a summer kitchen. Isn't that about it?"

She spread out the folds of her gown and looked down at them in a somewhat embarrassed manner, seemingly submerged by this flood of protesting eloquence.

"You were afraid to look anything in the face," he went on, not giving her time to recover her breath. "You thought you could live in a world of beauty and never have any hard work. I suppose if you had seen the gardener wiping the sweat off his brow you would not have picked any of the roses in that garden at Lucerne. I suppose not! Well, let me assure you of one thing-there's commonplaceness every-where. Probably some one had to wash those white dresses Sappho used to wear when she sat beside the sea. Maybe Sappho did them up herself, eh?"

He stopped and gave way to his bathos, throwing back his head and laughing heartily.

"Well, well, I'm through with railing at you. But I left you eating lotus, hollow-eyed and steeped in dreams. You were listening to the surf on Calypso's Isle. I was hearing nothing but the sound of your voice. Now I've stumbled on a soporific philosophy, and am getting all I can out of the anaesthesia, and you are reproaching me. It's like your inconsistency, isn't it?"

She put up one hand to stop him, but he went on, recurring once more to the poet:

"The Worldly Hope men set their Hearts upon
Turns Ashes--or it prospers; and anon,
Like snow upon the Desert's dusty Face
Lighting a little Hour or two, is gone."

She tried to speak, but he lifted his hat and left her, and going to the other side of the deck, paced up and down there swiftly, and thought of a number of things. For one thing, he reflected how ludicrous was life! Here was Helen Curtis, fleeing from the recollection of him; here was himself, fleeing from the too-sweet actuality of her calm face and lambent eyes; and they were set down face to face in midocean! Such a preposterous trick on the part of the Three!

"I suppose happiness is never anything more than a mirage," he said to himself as he paced. "It is bright at times and then dim, and at present, for me, it is inverted. The business of the traveller, however, is to tramp on in the sun and the sand, with an eye to the compass and giving no heed to evanishing gleams of fairy lakes and plumelike palms. Tramping on in the sand isn't as bad as it might be, either, when one gets used to it. The simoon is on me now, but I'll weather it. I've **got** to. I **won't be** downed!"

He put his head up and tried to think he was courageous. The gloom of the night was about him now, and the strange voices of the sea called one to the other. He tried to turn his thought to practical things. He would go home to the vacant old house where he had been born; he would make it livable, let the sunshine into it, modernize it to an extent, and then get some one under its roof. While there were so many homeless folk in the world it wasn't right to have an untenanted house. Then he'd get down to business, good and hard, and bring the thing up. It was a good business, and it had an honorable reputation. He had been too unappreciative of this fine legacy. Well, there were excuses. At school he had thought of other things--and the life of the fraternity house had been a gallant one! Then came his wander year--which stretched into two. And now, having eaten of the apples of Paradise and felt them turn to bitterness in his mouth, he would go back to duty.

He wished he had never seen her again--after that night when she belied her long-continued kindness to him with her indifferent rejection of his devotion. He devoutly wished he had not been forced to feel again the subtle fascination of those deep eyes, and hear the thrilling contralto of that rich voice! She was unscrupulous in her cold selfishness--

A sudden, inexplicable trembling of the whole great ship! A frightened quivering, a lurch, a crash!

The chug-chug ceased. No--it couldn't! Nothing like that ever happened to a ship of the line on a comparatively quiet night! Of course not!

Of course not--but for all of that, they were as inert as a raft, and the passengers were beginning to skurry about and to ask the third officer and the fourth officer what t' dickens it meant. The third officer and the fourth officer did not know, but felt convinced--professionally convinced--that it was nothing. The first engineer? He had gone below. Oh, it was nothing. The captain? Really, they could not say where he was.

Chalmers Payne strode around the after-cabin, and then ran to the spot where he had left Helen Curtis. She was still there. She sat up and put both her hands in his.

"I knew you'd be here as soon as you could, so I didn't move! I didn't want to put you to the trouble to look for me!"

He held her hands hard.

"I don't think it is much of anything," he said. "It can't be. There's no smell of fire. The sea is not heavy. At the very worst--"

"Be sure, won't you, that we're not separated? One of us might be put in one boat and one in another, you know, if it should really be--be fire or something. Then, if a storm came up and--"

People were running with vague rumors. They called out this and that alarm. It was possible to feel the panic gathering.

"Remember," Helen Curtis whispered, "whatever comes, that we belong together."

"We do!" he acquiesced, saying the words between his teeth. "I have known it a long time. But you--"

"Oh, so have I! But what made you so sure? What was there about your home and your work and yourself to make you so perfectly sure I would be interested in them all my life? You didn't lay out any scheme for me at all, or act as if you thought I had any dreams or aspirations. I was to come and observe you become distinguished--I was to watch what you could do! Oh, Chalmers, I was willing, but what made you so sure?"

"Then you loved me? You loved me?" She looked white and scared, and he could feel her hands chill and tremble.

"How ready you are to use that word! I'm afraid of it. I always said I wouldn't speak it till I **had** to. It frightens me--it means so much. If I said it to you I could never say it to any one else, no matter how--"

"Not on any account! Say it, Helen!"

"I wish to explain. I--I couldn't stand the aimlessness of life after you left. I began to suspect that it was you who made everything so interesting. I wasn't so enamoured with the ancients as I thought I was; but I was enamoured with your contemplation of my pose. Oh, I've been dissecting myself! Should I really have cared so much for Lucerne and Nuremberg if you hadn't been with me? I concluded that I should not. Well, said I to myself, if he can make the Old World so fascinating, can he not do something for the New World, too?"

An alarmist rushed by.

"They are going to lower the boats!" he cried. "Better get your valuables together."

"There's a panic in the steerage," another cried.

"Oh, Helen! Go on. Don't let anything interrupt you."

"I won't. I realize that you ought to be told that I love you. I do. I love you. I'm twenty-three, and I never said the words to any one else, even though I'm an American girl. And I'll never speak them to any one but you. I'm sure of it now. But I wouldn't say it till I was quite, quite sure."

The captain came pacing down the deck leisurely. He lifted his hat as he passed Payne and Miss Curtis.

"We shall be on our way in a few minutes," he said, agreeably. "I hope this young lady has not suffered any alarm."

Helen showed him a face on which anything was written rather than fear.

"The port shaft broke off somewhere near the truss-block at the mouth of the sleeve of the shaft, and the outer end of the shaft and the propeller dropped to the bottom of the sea. It's quite inexplicable, but I find in my experience that inexplicable things frequently happen. We shall finish our run with the starboard shaft only, and shall be obliged to reduce our speed to an average of three hundred and sixty knots daily."

He repeated this in a voice of impersonal courtesy, and went on to the next group. Helen Curtis settled back in her chair and smiled up at her lover.

"We shall be at sea at least two days longer," he said, exultantly.

"Ah, what shall we do to pass the time?" she interrupted, with mocking coquetry.

"Chug-chug, chug-chug!"

It was the liner.

"Ah, my Beloved, fill the Cup that clears

To-day of past Regret and future Fears--"

This was Omar, but Miss Curtis would not listen.

"I've an aversion to your eloquent old heathen," she pleaded. "You must not quote him, really."

"If you insist, I'll refrain. Can't I even quote 'A book of verses underneath the bough--'"

"Oh, not on any account! That least of all."

"You don't want me to be hackneyed? Well, I'll be perfectly original. I know one thing I can say which will always sound mysterious and marvellous!"

"Say it, say it!" she commanded, imperiously, knowing quite well what it was.

So he said it, and the two sat and looked off across the darkened water and at the pale, reluctant stars, beholding, for that night at least, the passionate inner sense of the universe. They said nothing more.

But as for the liner, it continued with its emphatic reiteration.

THE MINISTER
ANNIE HAMILTON DONNELL

Mrs. Leah Bloodgood walked heavily, without the painstaking little springy leaps she usually adopted as an offset to her stoutness. She mounted Cornelia Opp's door-steps with an air of gloomy abstraction that sat uneasily on the plump terraces of her face as if at any moment it might slide off. It slid off now at sight of Cornelia Opp's serene, sweet face.

"My gracious! Cornelia, is this your house?" laughed Mrs. Bloodgood, pantingly. "Here I thought I was going up Marilla Merritt's steps! You don't mean to tell me that I turned into Ridgway Street instead of Penn?"

"This isn't Penn Street," smiled Cornelia Opp. She had flung the door wide with a gesture of welcome.

"No--mercy, no, I can't come in!" panted the woman on the steps. "I've got to see Marilla Merritt, right off. When I come calling on *you*, Cornelia, I want my mind easy so we can have a good time."

"Poor Mrs. Merritt!"

"Well, Marilla ought to suffer if I do--she's on the Suffering Committee! Good-by, Cornelia. Don't you go and tell anybody how absent-minded I was. They'll say it's catching."

"It's the minister, then," mused Cornelia in the doorway, watching the stout figure go down the street. "Now what has the poor man been doing this time?" A gentle pity grew in her beautiful gray eyes. It was so hard on ministers to be all alone in the world, especially certain kinds of ministers. No matter how long-suffering Suffering Committees might be, they could not make allowances *enough*. "Poor man! Well, the Lord's on his side," smiled in the doorway Cornelia Opp.

Marilla Merritt was not like Mrs. Leah Bloodgood. Marilla was little where

Leah was big, and nothing daunted Marilla. She was shaking a rug out on her sunny piazza, and descried the toiling figure while it was yet afar off.

"There's Leah Bloodgood coming, or my name's Sarah! **What** is Leah Bloodgood out this time of day for, with the minister's dinner to get? Something is up." She waved the rug gayly. "Mis' Merritt isn't at home!" she called; "she's out--on the door-steps shaking rugs! Leah Bloodgood," as the figure drew near, "you look all tuckered out! Come in quick and sit down. Don't try to talk. You needn't tell me something's up--just say *what*. Has that blessed man been--"

"Yes, he has!" panted the caller, vindictively. It is harder to be long-suffering when one is out of breath. "You listen to this. I've brought his letter to read to you."

"His letter!" Marilla could not have been much more astonished if the other had taken the minister himself out of her dangling black bag.

"Yes; it came this morn--Mercy! Marilla, don't look so amazed! Didn't you know he'd gone away on his vacation? He forgot it was next month instead of this, and I found him packing his things, and hadn't the heart to tell him. I thought a man with a pleased look like that on his face better *go*,--but, mercy! didn't I send you word? It *is* catching. I shall be bad as he is."

"Good as he is, do you mean? Don't worry about being that!" laughed little Marilla Merritt. "Well, I'm glad he's gone, dear man."

"You won't be glad long, 'dear man'! Here's his letter. Take a long breath before you read it. I suppose I ought to prepare you, but I want you see how I felt."

"I might count ten first," deliberated smiling Marilla, fingering the white envelope with a certain tenderness. A certain tenderness and the minister went together with them all. "But, no, I'm going to sail right in."

"Take your own risks, of course, but my advice is to reef all your main--er--jib-sails first," Mrs. Leah Bloodgood wearily murmured. "You'll find the sea choppy."

"'Dear Sister Bloodgood,'" read Marilla, aloud, with reckless glibness, "'Will you be so kind as to send me my best suit? I am going to marry my old friend whom I have met here after twenty years. The wedding will take place next Wednesday morn--'

"What!"

"Read on," groaned Mrs. Bloodgood. "He says the fishing's excellent."

"I should say so! And that's what he's caught! Leah Bloodgood, what did you ever let him go away for without a body-guard? That poor dear, innocent, kind-hearted man, to go and fall among--among *thieves* like that!"

"He's just absent-minded enough to go and do it himself. I don't suppose we ought to blame *them*. Read on."

"'Next Wednesday morning, at ten o'clock,'" moaned little Marilla, glibness all gone. "'It would be most embarrassing to do so in these clothes, as I am sure you will see, dear sister. Kindly see that my best white tie is included. I would not wish to be unbecomingly attired on so joyous an occasion. She is a widow with five chil--'"

"Mercy! don't faint away! Where's your fans? Didn't I tell you there were breakers ahead? I don't wonder you're all broken up! Give it to me; I'll read the rest. M--m--m, 'joyous occasion'--'five children'--'she is a widow with five children, all of them most lovable little creatures. You know my fondness for children. I have been greatly benefited by my sojourn in this lovely spot. I cannot thank you too warmly for recommending it. I find the fish--'"

"Leah Bloodgood, that will do! Don't read another word. Don't fan me, don't ask me how I feel now. Let me get my breath, and then we will go over and open the parsonage windows. That, I suppose, is the first thing to do. It's something to be thankful for that it's a good-sized parsonage."

"Be thankful, then--I'm not. I'm not anything but incensed clear through. After I'd taken every precaution that was ever thought of, and some that weren't ever, to keep that man out of mischief! I thought of all the absent-minded things he might do, but I never thought of this, no, I never! And we wanted him to marry Cornelia so much, Marilla! Cornelia would have made him such a beautiful wife!"

"Beautiful!" sighed Marilla, hopelessly. It had been the dear pet plan they had nursed in common with all the parish. Everybody but the minister and Cornelia had shared in it.

"And five children! Marilla Merritt, think of five children romping over our parsonage, knocking all the corners off!"

"I'm thinking," mourned Marilla, gustily. She felt a dismal suspicion that this was going to daunt her. But her habit of facing things came to the front. "Wednesday's only four days off," she said, with a fine assumption of briskness. "I don't suppose he said anything about a wedding tour, did he?"

"No. But even if he took one he'd probably forget and stop off here. So we can't count on that. What's done has got to be done in four days. What **has** got to be done, Marilla?"

"Everything. We must start this minute, Leah Bloodgood! The house must be aired and painted and papered, and window-glass set--there's no end! And all in four days! We can't let our minister bring his wife and five children home to a shabby house. Cornelia Opp must go round and get money for new dining-room chairs, and there ought to be more beds with a family like that. Dishes, too. Cornelia ought to start at **once**. She's the best solicitor we have."

"There's another thing," broke out Mrs. Bloodgood; "the minister must have some new shirts. He ought to have a whole trousseau. He hasn't boarded with me, and I done all his mending, without my knowing what he ought to have, now that he's going to go and get married. We can't let **him** be shabby, either."

"Then, of course, there ought to be a lot of cooked food in the house, and supper all ready for them when they come. Oh, I guess we'll find plenty to do! I guess we can't stop to groan much. But, oh, how different we'd all feel if it was Cornelia!"

"Different! I'd give 'em my dining-room chairs and my cellar stairs! I'd make shirts and sit up all night to cook! It's--it's wicked, Marilla, that's what it is."

"I know **it** is, but he isn't," championed Marilla. "He's just a good man gone wrong. It's his guardian angel that's to blame--a guardian angel has no business to be napping."

At best, it was pretty late in the day to overhaul a parsonage that had been closed so long and sinking gently into mild decay. The little parish woke with a dismayed start and went to work, to a woman. Operations were begun within an amazingly brief time; cleaners and repairers were hurried to the parsonage, and the women of the parish were told off into relays to assist them.

"Somebody go to Mrs. Higginbotham Taylor's and get a high chair," directed Marilla Merritt. "I'll lend my tea-chair for the next-to-the-baby, anyway, till they can get something better. We don't want our minister's children sitting round on dictionaries and encyclopaedias."

The minister had come to them, a lone bachelor, with kind, absent eyes and the faculty of making himself beloved. For six years they had taken care of him and loved him--watched over his outgoings and his incomings and forgiven all his absent-mindednesses. They had picked out Cornelia Opp for him, and added it to their prayers like an earnest codicil--"O Lord, bring Cornelia Opp and the minister together. Amen."

Cornelia Opp herself lived on her sweet, unselfish, single life, and prayed, "Lord, bless the minister," unsuspectingly. She was as much beloved among them all as the minister. They were proud of her slender, beautiful figure and her serene face, and of her many capabilities. What the minister lacked, Cornelia had; Cornelia lacked nothing.

Marilla Merritt and Cornelia Opp were appointed receiving committee, to be at the parsonage when the minister and his wife and five children arrived. A bountiful supper was to be in readiness, prepared by all the good women impartially. The duty of the receiving committee was merely, as Mrs. Leah Bloodgood said, "to smile, and tell pleasant little lies--'Such a delightful surprise,--so glad to welcome, etc.'

"Cornelia and Marilla Merritt are just the ones," she said, succinctly. "I should say: 'You awful man, you! Can't we trust you out of our sights?' And I suppose that wouldn't be the best way to welcome 'em."

The minister had sent a brief notice of his expected arrival home on Wednesday evening, and, unless he forgot and went somewhere else, there was good reason to expect him then. Everything was hurried into readiness. At the last moment some one sent in a doll to make the minister's children feel more at home. Cornelia laughed and set the little thing on the sofa, stiffly erect and endlessly smiling.

"Looks nice, doesn't it?" sighed tired little Marilla, returning from a last round of the tidy rooms. "I don't see anything else left to do, unless--Is that dust?"

"No, it's bloom," hastened Cornelia, covertly wiping it off. "You poor, tired thing, don't look at anything else! Just go home and rest a little bit before you change your dress. Mine's all changed, and I can stay here and mount guard. I can be practising my lies!"

"I've got mine by heart," laughed Marilla, "I could say 'so delighted' if he brought two wives and ten children!"

"Don't!" Cornelia's sweet voice sounded a little severe. "We've said enough about the poor man. It's four o'clock. If you're going--"

"I am. Cornelia Opp, turn that child back to! She makes me nervous sitting there on that sofa staring at me! Will you see her!"

"She does look a little out of place," Cornelia admitted, but she left the stiff little figure undisturbed. After the other woman had gone she sat down beside it on the sofa, and smoothed absently its gaudy little dress. Cornelia's face was gently pensive, she could scarcely have told why. Not the minister, but the trimly appointed house with its indefinable atmosphere of a home with little children in it was what she was thinking of without conscious effort of her own. The smiling doll beside her, the high chair that she could see through an inner door, and the foolish little gilt mug that some one had donated to the minister's babyest one--they all contributed to the gentle pensiveness on Cornelia's sweet face. She was but a step by thirty, and a woman at thirty has not settled down resignedly into a lonely old age. Let a little child come tilting by, or a little child's foolish belongings intrude themselves upon her vision, and old, odd longings creep out of secret crannies and haunt her, willy-nilly. It is the latent motherhood within her that has been denied its own. It was the secret of the soft wistfulness in Cornelia's eyes. So she sat until the minister came home. It was the sound of his big step on the walk that roused her and sent the color into her face and made it perilously beautiful.

Cornelia was frightened. Where was Marilla Merritt? Why had they come so soon? Must she meet them alone? She hurried to the door, her perturbed mind groping blindly for the "lies" she had misplaced while she sat and dreamed.

The minister was striding up the walk alone! He did not even look back at the village hack that was turning away with his wife and five children! He looked instead at the beautiful vision that stood in the parsonage doorway, glimpses of home behind it, welcome and comfort in it. The minister was in need of welcome and comfort. His loneliness had been accentuated cruelly by the bit of happiness he had caught a brief glimpse of and left behind him. Perhaps the loneliness was in his face.

"Welcome home," Cornelia said, in the doorway. She put aside her astonishment at his coming alone, and answered the need in his face. Her hands were out in a gracious greeting. To the minister how good it was!

"They told me to come right here," he said, "or I should have gone to Mrs. Bloodgood's as usual. I don't quite understand--"

"Never mind understanding," Cornelia smiled, leading the way into the pretty parlor, "anyway, till you get into a comfortable rocker. It's so much easier to understand in a rocking-chair! I--well, I think I need one, too! You see, we expected--we ***didn't*** expect you alone."

"No?" his puzzled gaze taking in all the kind little appointments of the room, and coming to a stop at the smiling doll. The two of them sat and stared at each other.

"We thought you would bring--we got all ready for your wife and the children," Cornelia was saying. The doll stared on, but the minister looked up.

"My wife and the children?" he repeated after her. "I don't think I know what you mean, Miss Cornelia. I must be dreaming--No, wait; please don't tell me what it all means just yet! Give me a little time to enjoy the dream." But Cornelia went on.

"You wrote Mrs. Bloodgood about your marriage," she said. Sweet voices can be severe. "It hurried us a little, but we have tried to get everything in readiness. If there is another bed needed for the chil--"

"I wrote Mrs. Bloodgood about my marriage?" he said, slowly; then as understanding dawned upon him the puzzled lines in his face loosened into laughter that would out. He leaned back in his rocker and gave himself up to it helplessly. As helplessly Cornelia joined in. The doll on the sofa smiled on--no more, no less.

"Will you ex--excuse me?" he laughed.

"No," laughed she.

"But I can't help it, and you're l-laughing yourself."

"No!"

He got to his feet and caught her hands.

"Let's keep on," he pleaded, unministerially. "I'm having a beautiful time. Aren't you? I wish you'd say yes, Miss Cornelia!"

"Yes," she smiled, "but we can't sit here laughing all the rest of the afternoon. Marilla Merritt will be here--"

"Oh, Marilla Merritt--" He sighed. The minister was young, too.

"And she will want to know--things," hinted Cornelia, mildly. She drew the smiling doll into her lap and smoothed its dress absently. The minister retreated to his rocker again.

"I think I would rather tell you," he said, quietly. "I did marry my old friend this morning, but I married her to another man. It was a mistake--all a mistake."

"Then you ought not to have married her, ought you?" commented Cornelia, demurely. Over the doll's little foolish head her eyes were dancing. Marilla Merritt might not see that it was funny, Mrs. Bloodgood mightn't, but it was. Unless--unless it was pathetic. Suddenly Cornelia felt that it was.

The minister was no longer laughing. He sat in the rocker strangely quiet. Perhaps he did not realize that his eyes were on Cornelia's beautiful face; perhaps he thought he was looking at the doll. He knew what he was thinking of. The utter loneliness behind him and ahead of him appalled him in its contrast to this. This woman sitting opposite him with the face of the woman that a man would like always near him, this little home with the two of them in it alone--the minister knew what it was he wanted. He wanted it to go right on--never to end. He knew that he had always wanted it. All the soul of the man rose up to claim it. And because there was need of hurry, because Marilla Merritt was coming, he held out his hands to Cornelia and the foolish, unastonished doll.

"Come," he said, pleadingly, and of course the doll could not have gone alone. He dropped it gently back into its place on the sofa.

Marilla Merritt had been unwarrantably delayed. She came in flushed and panting, but indomitably smiling. Her sharp glance sought for a wife and five children.

"Such a delightful surprise!" she panted, holding out her hand to the minister. "We are so glad to welcome--Why!--have you shown them to their rooms, Cornelia?"

"They--they didn't come," murmured Cornelia, retreating to her unfailing ally on the sofa. In the stress of the moment--for Cornelia was not ready for Marilla Merritt--it had seemed to her that the time for "lies" had come. She had even beckoned to the nearest one. But the ghosts of ministers' wives that had been and that were to be had risen in a warning cloud about her and saved her.

"Didn't come!" shrilled Marilla Merritt in her astonishment. "His wife and children didn't come! Do you know what you are saying, Cornelia? You don't mean-- Then I don't wonder you look flustered--" She caught herself up hurriedly, but her thoughts ran on unchecked. Of all things that ever! Could absent-mindedness go further than this--to marry a wife and forget to bring her home with him?--and *five children!*

Marilla Merritt turned sharply upon the minister.

"Where is your wife?" she demanded, the frayed ends of her patience trailing from her tone. The minister crossed the room to Cornelia and the doll. He laid his big white hand gently on Cornelia's small white one. There was protective tenderness in the gesture and the touch.

"I found her here waiting for me," the minister said.

The Codes Of Hammurabi And Moses
W. W. Davies

QTY

The discovery of the Hammurabi Code is one of the greatest achievements of archaeology, and is of paramount interest, not only to the student of the Bible, but also to all those interested in ancient history...

Religion   **ISBN:** *1-59462-338-4*   Pages:132
MSRP $12.95

The Theory of Moral Sentiments
Adam Smith

QTY

This work from 1749. contains original theories of conscience amd moral judgment and it is the foundation for systemof morals.

Philosophy **ISBN:** *1-59462-777-0*   Pages:536
MSRP $19.95

Jessica's First Prayer
Hesba Stretton

QTY

In a screened and secluded corner of one of the many railway-bridges which span the streets of London there could be seen a few years ago, from five o'clock every morning until half past eight, a tidily set-out coffee-stall, consisting of a trestle and board, upon which stood two large tin cans, with a small fire of charcoal burning under each so as to keep the coffee boiling during the early hours of the morning when the work-people were thronging into the city on their way to their daily toil...

Childrens   **ISBN:** *1-59462-373-2*   Pages:84
MSRP $9.95

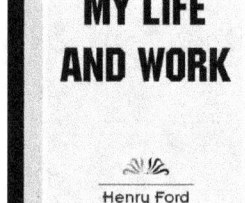

My Life and Work
Henry Ford

QTY

Henry Ford revolutionized the world with his implementation of mass production for the Model T automobile. Gain valuable business insight into his life and work with his own auto-biography... "We have only started on our development of our country we have not as yet, with all our talk of wonderful progress, done more than scratch the surface. The progress has been wonderful enough but..."

Biographies/ **ISBN:** *1-59462-198-5*   Pages:300
MSRP $21.95

The Art of Cross-Examination
Francis Wellman

QTY

I presume it is the experience of every author, after his first book is published upon an important subject, to be almost overwhelmed with a wealth of ideas and illustrations which could readily have been included in his book, and which to his own mind, at least, seem to make a second edition inevitable. Such certainly was the case with me; and when the first edition had reached its sixth impression in five months, I rejoiced to learn that it seemed to my publishers that the book had met with a sufficiently favorable reception to justify a second and considerably enlarged edition. ..

Pages:412

Reference   **ISBN: *1-59462-647-2***   *MSRP $19.95*

On the Duty of Civil Disobedience
Henry David Thoreau

QTY

Thoreau wrote his famous essay, On the Duty of Civil Disobedience, as a protest against an unjust but popular war and the immoral but popular institution of slave-owning. He did more than write—he declined to pay his taxes, and was hauled off to gaol in consequence. Who can say how much this refusal of his hastened the end of the war and of slavery ?

Law   **ISBN: *1-59462-747-9***   **Pages:48**

MSRP $7.45

Dream Psychology Psychoanalysis for Beginners
Sigmund Freud

QTY

Sigmund Freud, born Sigismund Schlomo Freud (May 6, 1856 - September 23, 1939), was a Jewish-Austrian neurologist and psychiatrist who co-founded the psychoanalytic school of psychology. Freud is best known for his theories of the unconscious mind, especially involving the mechanism of repression; his redefinition of sexual desire as mobile and directed towards a wide variety of objects; and his therapeutic techniques, especially his understanding of transference in the therapeutic relationship and the presumed value of dreams as sources of insight into unconscious desires.

Pages:196

Psychology   **ISBN: *1-59462-905-6***   *MSRP $15.45*

The Miracle of Right Thought
Orison Swett Marden

QTY

Believe with all of your heart that you will do what you were made to do. When the mind has once formed the habit of holding cheerful, happy, prosperous pictures, it will not be easy to form the opposite habit. It does not matter how improbable or how far away this realization may see, or how dark the prospects may be, if we visualize them as best we can, as vividly as possible, hold tenaciously to them and vigorously struggle to attain them, they will gradually become actualized, realized in the life. But a desire, a longing without endeavor, a yearning abandoned or held indifferently will vanish without realization.

Pages:360

Self Help   **ISBN: *1-59462-644-8***   *MSRP $25.45*

QTY

The Rosicrucian Cosmo-Conception Mystic Christianity *by Max Heindel* ISBN: *1-59462-188-8* **$38.95**
The Rosicrucian Cosmo-conception is not dogmatic, neither does it appeal to any other authority than the reason of the student. It is: not controversial, but is: sent forth in the, hope that it may help to clear... *New Age/Religion Pages 646*

Abandonment To Divine Providence *by Jean-Pierre de Caussade* ISBN: *1-59462-228-0* **$25.95**
"The Rev. Jean Pierre de Caussade was one of the most remarkable spiritual writers of the Society of Jesus in France in the 18th Century. His death took place at Toulouse in 1751. His works have gone through many editions and have been republished... *Inspirational/Religion Pages 400*

Mental Chemistry *by Charles Haanel* ISBN: *1-59462-192-6* **$23.95**
Mental Chemistry allows the change of material conditions by combining and appropriately utilizing the power of the mind. Much like applied chemistry creates something new and unique out of careful combinations of chemicals the mastery of mental chemistry... *New Age Pages 354*

The Letters of Robert Browning and Elizabeth Barret Barrett 1845-1846 vol II ISBN: *1-59462-193-4* **$35.95**
by Robert Browning and Elizabeth Barrett *Biographies Pages 596*

Gleanings In Genesis (volume I) *by Arthur W. Pink* ISBN: *1-59462-130-6* **$27.45**
Appropriately has Genesis been termed "the seed plot of the Bible" for in it we have, in germ form, almost all of the great doctrines which are afterwards fully developed in the books of Scripture which follow... *Religion/Inspirational Pages 420*

The Master Key *by L. W. de Laurence* ISBN: *1-59462-001-6* **$30.95**
In no branch of human knowledge has there been a more lively increase of the spirit of research during the past few years than in the study of Psychology, Concentration and Mental Discipline. The requests for authentic lessons in Thought Control, Mental Discipline and... *New Age/Business Pages 422*

The Lesser Key Of Solomon Goetia *by L. W. de Laurence* ISBN: *1-59462-092-X* **$9.95**
This translation of the first book of the "Lernegton" which is now for the first time made accessible to students of Talismanic Magic was done, after careful collation and edition, from numerous Ancient Manuscripts in Hebrew, Latin, and French... *New Age/Occult Pages 92*

Rubaiyat Of Omar Khayyam *by Edward Fitzgerald* ISBN: *1-59462-332-5* **$13.95**
Edward Fitzgerald, whom the world has already learned, in spite of his own efforts to look upon within the shadow of anonymity, to look upon as one of the rarest poets of the century, was born at Bredfield, in Suffolk, on the 31st of March, 1809. He was the third son of John Purcell... *Music Pages 172*

Ancient Law *by Henry Maine* ISBN: *1-59462-128-4* **$29.95**
The chief object of the following pages is to indicate some of the earliest ideas of mankind, as they are reflected in Ancient Law, and to point out the relation of those ideas to modern thought. *Religiom/History Pages 452*

Far-Away Stories *by William J. Locke* ISBN: *1-59462-129-2* **$19.45**
"Good wine needs no bush, but a collection of mixed vintages does. And this book is just such a collection. Some of the stories I do not want to remain buried for ever in the museum files of dead magazine-numbers an author's not unpardonable vanity..." *Fiction Pages 272*

Life of David Crockett *by David Crockett* ISBN: *1-59462-250-7* **$27.45**
"Colonel David Crockett was one of the most remarkable men of the times in which he lived. Born in humble life, but gifted with a strong will, an indomitable courage, and unremitting perseverance... *Biographies/New Age Pages 424*

Lip-Reading *by Edward Nitchie* ISBN: *1-59462-206-X* **$25.95**
Edward B. Nitchie, founder of the New York School for the Hard of Hearing, now the Nitchie School of Lip-Reading, Inc, wrote "LIP-READING Principles and Practice". The development and perfecting of this meritorious work on lip-reading was an undertaking... *How-to Pages 400*

A Handbook of Suggestive Therapeutics, Applied Hypnotism, Psychic Science ISBN: *1-59462-214-0* **$24.95**
by Henry Munro *Health/New Age/Health/Self-help Pages 376*

A Doll's House: and Two Other Plays *by Henrik Ibsen* ISBN: *1-59462-112-8* **$19.95**
Henrik Ibsen created this classic when in revolutionary 1848 Rome. Introducing some striking concepts in playwriting for the realist genre, this play has been studied the world over. *Fiction/Classics/Plays 308*

The Light of Asia *by sir Edwin Arnold* ISBN: *1-59462-204-3* **$13.95**
In this poetic masterpiece, Edwin Arnold describes the life and teachings of Buddha. The man who was to become known as Buddha to the world was born as Prince Gautama of India but he rejected the worldly riches and abandoned the reigns of power when... *Religion/History/Biographies Pages 170*

The Complete Works of Guy de Maupassant *by Guy de Maupassant* ISBN: *1-59462-157-8* **$16.95**
"For days and days, nights and nights, I had dreamed of that first kiss which was to consecrate our engagement, and I knew not on what spot I should put my lips..." *Fiction/Classics Pages 240*

The Art of Cross-Examination *by Francis L. Wellman* ISBN: *1-59462-309-0* **$26.95**
Written by a renowned trial lawyer, Wellman imparts his experience and uses case studies to explain how to use psychology to extract desired information through questioning. *How-to/Science/Reference Pages 408*

Answered or Unanswered? *by Louisa Vaughan* ISBN: *1-59462-248-5* **$10.95**
Miracles of Faith in China *Religion Pages 112*

The Edinburgh Lectures on Mental Science (1909) *by Thomas* ISBN: *1-59462-008-3* **$11.95**
This book contains the substance of a course of lectures recently given by the writer in the Queen Street Hail, Edinburgh. Its purpose is to indicate the Natural Principles governing the relation between Mental Action and Material Conditions... *New Age/Psychology Pages 148*

Ayesha *by H. Rider Haggard* ISBN: *1-59462-301-5* **$24.95**
Verily and indeed it is the unexpected that happens! Probably if there was one person upon the earth from whom the Editor of this, and of a certain previous history, did not expect to hear again... *Classics Pages 380*

Ayala's Angel *by Anthony Trollope* ISBN: *1-59462-352-X* **$29.95**
The two girls were both pretty, but Lucy who was twenty-one who supposed to be simple and comparatively unattractive, whereas Ayala was credited, as her Bombwhat romantic name might show, with poetic charm and a taste for romance. Ayala when her father died was nineteen... *Fiction Pages 484*

The American Commonwealth *by James Bryce* ISBN: *1-59462-286-8* **$34.45**
An interpretation of American democratic political theory. It examines political mechanics and society from the perspective of Scotsman James Bryce *Politics Pages 572*

Stories of the Pilgrims *by Margaret P. Pumphrey* ISBN: *1-59462-116-0* **$17.95**
This book explores pilgrims religious oppression in England as well as their escape to Holland and eventual crossing to America on the Mayflower, and their early days in New England... *History Pages 268*

QTY

The Fasting Cure *by Sinclair Upton*　　　　　　　　　　　　　ISBN: *1-59462-222-1*　**$13.95**
In the Cosmopolitan Magazine for May, 1910, and in the Contemporary Review (London) for April, 1910, I published an article dealing with my experiences in fasting. I have written a great many magazine articles, but never one which attracted so much attention... New Age/Self Help/Health Pages 164

Hebrew Astrology *by Sepharial*　　　　　　　　　　　　　　ISBN: *1-59462-308-2*　**$13.45**
In these days of advanced thinking it is a matter of common observation that we have left many of the old landmarks behind and that we are now pressing forward to greater heights and to a wider horizon than that which represented the mind-content of our progenitors... Astrology Pages 144

Thought Vibration or The Law of Attraction in the Thought World　　ISBN: *1-59462-127-6*　**$12.95**

by William Walker Atkinson　　　　　　　　　　　　　　　　　*Psychology/Religion Pages 144*

Optimism *by Helen Keller*　　　　　　　　　　　　　　　　ISBN: *1-59462-108-X*　**$15.95**
Helen Keller was blind, deaf, and mute since 19 months old, yet famously learned how to overcome these handicaps, communicate with the world, and spread her lectures promoting optimism. An inspiring read for everyone... Biographies/Inspirational Pages 84

Sara Crewe *by Frances Burnett*　　　　　　　　　　　　　　ISBN: *1-59462-360-0*　**$9.45**
In the first place, Miss Minchin lived in London. Her home was a large, dull, tall one, in a large, dull square, where all the houses were alike, and all the sparrows were alike, and where all the door-knockers made the same heavy sound... Childrens/Classic Pages 88

The Autobiography of Benjamin Franklin *by Benjamin Franklin*　　ISBN: *1-59462-135-7*　**$24.95**
The Autobiography of Benjamin Franklin has probably been more extensively read than any other American historical work, and no other book of its kind has had such ups and downs of fortune. Franklin lived for many years in England, where he was agent... Biographies/History Pages 332

Name	
Email	
Telephone	
Address	
City, State ZIP	

☐ **Credit Card**　　　　　☐ **Check / Money Order**

Credit Card Number	
Expiration Date	
Signature	

Please Mail to:　Book Jungle
PO Box 2226
Champaign, IL 61825
or Fax to:　　　630-214-0564

ORDERING INFORMATION
web: *www.bookjungle.com*
email: *sales@bookjungle.com*
fax: *630-214-0564*
mail: *Book Jungle PO Box 2226 Champaign, IL 61825*
or PayPal *to sales@bookjungle.com*

Please contact us for bulk discounts

DIRECT-ORDER TERMS

**20% Discount if You Order
Two or More Books**
Free Domestic Shipping!
Accepted: Master Card, Visa,
Discover, American Express